Journey in Providence

A Theological Novel

Behind a frowning providence,
He hides a smiling face.

1) Please read this book with an open Bible. The only Inspired and infallible guide to God's people is the Bible.

2) Please return this book to Providence Reformed Baptist Church so others may benefit from it as well.

Richard P. Belcher

Cover Photography by Ravenel Scott

ISBN 1-883265-19-3

Richbarry Press

P.O. Box 302   **Columbia, SC 29202**
Phone: 803-750-0408
E-Mail: docbelcher@juno.com

Printed in the Unites States of America

Contents

Index to Scripture Exposition
(The page given is the page where the exposition begins)

Am I Prepared for This...?

It is the very time for faith, when sight ceases.
George Mueller

For those of you who have taken previous journeys with us, as well as for new travelers, let me give you the background of this present embarkation into the realm of theological truth.

These journeys began in 1970 as I was a student in college studying for the ministry. The last journey was in the fall of 1976 as I went to seminary. The present pursuit begins five years later in the summer of 1981. I had by then finished the Master of Divinity, and was taking a break from school before going on to a further degree.

As pastor of Unity Baptist Church, I was enjoying the summer and freedom from papers, exams, and all the other pressures of schooling. I had planned to spend about a year "cooling down" from student life before beginning the next educational step. I was beginning to sense a desire to teach someday in a college or seminary, but for now I was badly in need of time with family and church, along with some recuperation.

I had no idea that I was about to begin another of those "searches" for truth into which the Lord had plunged me previously. But most shocking was the event that launched me into what was to become the most difficult and painful journey yet. Who can anticipate the events of one day or one hour?

It all began on one of those well-known hot, muggy, sweaty summer days of our area. The temperature must have been over a hundred degrees. Even the breeze, what there was of it, seemed to be hiding from the heat. And when one did feel it, it was scorching instead of refreshing. It was one of those days when, if you did not have air conditioning in your car, you were more comfortable with the window up, because the heat pouring in was oppressive and scalding.

I had been to the hospital in the early afternoon, and had just returned to my air-conditioned church office to take refuge in my sermon preparation for the next Lord's day. Then the phone resounded with its normal interrupting jangle. As I picked it up, I expected some small, minor, insignificant situation, but it was far more than that--- perhaps the most shocking call I had ever received in my life.

"Pastor Ira? This is Troy Medford. You had better come quickly. Dink and Janie need you badly!"

Troy and Dink had both been saved during those early days at First Baptist Church. Troy was a member of my church and also served on the local police force. Dink was a real character and a former gang member. He had since graduated from college and seminary, and was on our church staff. Janie was his wife.

"Troy, this sounds very serious! Have they been in an accident?" I asked.

"No, worse than that!" he declared, and my mind began to wonder what could be worse than an automobile accident.

Then when Troy continued, there was no denying it---it was worse than an automobile accident.

"Little Dinky has been kidnapped!" Troy said, with his voice breaking, though he tried to keep his calm demeanor as a police officer. "I am with them at the Food Zone super market!"

"I'll be right there!" I blurted, almost hanging up the phone before finishing my sentence, as I was in such a hurry to get to them.

As I drove the few miles to Food Zone, I remembered how Dink had been saved during that difficult experience we had faced at First Baptist Church; how he had become such a strong witness for Christ, fearing no one; how he had grown as he studied and searched for the truth; how he had met Janie at First Baptist Church in the middle of the Durwood Girvin experience; how they were so different, as she was almost the opposite of Dink---shy, quiet, reserved, etc.; how they were married and then sent the gift of a son, Little Dinky, as Dink called him; how he and I had gone to seminary together, and the many times he had blown people away with his grasp of the truth though he still looked like and dressed somewhat like and talked like a gangster.

But now tragedy had struck---the most horrible kind--- the pride and joy of their lives had been taken from them (hopefully only temporarily).

As I turned into the Food Zone parking lot, I couldn't even begin to imagine what they were going through in this hour. I too had a son a little older than Little Dinky! What would I tell them in this hour? What could I tell them? At this moment I realized that all the years of schooling I had endured in readiness for the ministry had not prepared me for this moment!

And somehow, the heat no longer mattered!

Can You Explain This Tragic Mystery...?

Never should we so abandon ourselves to God,
as when He seems to have abandoned us.
Anonymous

As I turned into the Food Zone parking lot, it wasn't difficult to find Dink and Janie. Though the store itself was about a block off of the highway, the presence of police cars directed me immediately to them.   Dink and Janie were sitting in chairs that someone had provided, but when they saw me they rose and we embraced for a few moments as we stood crying together. It was the first time I had ever seen Dink, the converted tough guy and former gang leader, cry.

I noticed also that Dink looked like he had just been through a gang fight. His face was was cut and scratched, and his pants and shirt were torn and ripped, with some blood evident on them. Even his hands and arms were black and blue and skinned and cut.

Then I whispered to them, as we continued to embrace, some words of a poem I had learned several years previously.

My Father's way may twist and turn,
My heart may throb and ache.
But in my soul, I'm glad I know,
God maketh no mistake.

They both nodded in agreement with the truth of these words, but then Dink asked, "But why, preacha? Why?" With those words both he and Janie broke down and began to weep with open, engulfing and devasting sobs---the kind one tries to stop but cannot.

After a few moments of just hugging them, I replied, as they settled down, "We'll talk about that in the hours ahead, but right now we must walk by faith as did Job and so many other servants of God of old."

I could tell, though, that though they spoke agreement with the theology of the poem I had quoted, their hearts were still aching for an answer to that question of why. We prayed together and stood hoping for some word of Little Dinky's whereabouts.

As the next hour or so passed, I learned the details of what had taken place. Dink had gone to the Food Zone for some items, and had taken Little Dinky with him. When he came out, he started the car, turned on the air conditioning, rolled down a window, and put Little Dinky in the car to get cool while he walked the grocery cart back to the store---a distance of about 100 feet. After he had deposited the cart in its proper place, as he turned around he saw a man getting into his car.

He began to yell and scream at the guy, as he ran toward the car, and then seeing it beginning to move, he hurled himself onto the trunk, trying to hold on for dear life and maybe even the life of Little Dinky. He could see him in the back seat turning his head looking so pitifully at him. The driver weaved trying to throw Dink off, but was unsuccessful.

As they came to a place where the car had to slow down almost to a stop, Dink jumped off of the trunk, and lunged for the driver's door, but the car roared off again, this time with Dink grabbing the door of the open window of the back seat. As they shot down the busy highway Dink tried to climb inside the car. At one point he even grabbed the driver's hair, but had been slashed on his arm by a knife.

Finally he couldn't hold on any longer due to the continuing knife cuts. He unwantingly dropped to the highway, only to watch the car with Little Dinky fade into the distance, as he jumped to his feet and ran for several hundred yards after it. When he couldn't stop a passing car to help him in his chase, he fell despondantly to his knees on the side of the pavement, and wept, beating his cut and bruised hands on the ground in frustration and helplessness.

Then he came to his senses and rushed to the nearest phone and called the police. But by the time they arrived, the driver and kidnapper had at least a twenty to thirty minute headstart, and could have been miles away. The police put out an alert for his car, and then took him back to the Food Zone to get a detailed desciption of what had taken place.

We kept hoping word would come about the location of his car and the capture of the driver, but it seemed car, driver and Little Dinky had completely vanished.

As I waited with them, I was struck with the unexpectancy of the arrival of tragedy and sorrow. It is unpredictable, as it bursts in unannounced, uninvited, unwelcome, unwanted and unexplained, finding us unprepared and unwilling to accept it, though so often we have no choice in the matter.

Is there any theologian who can explain it thoroughly? Is there any philsopher who holds the key to its mystery? Is there any man who can face its cruel assault and not shudder from its crushing blows? Even as we are committed to the truth that God holds the key to these crashing moments of sorrow, we must also admit that He does not always give us the key to unlock immediately the deep mystery of sorrow. He gives us faith to trust Him, and the question is, will that be enough for the hour of our bewilderment and sorrow?

Or will we foolishly demand that the omniscient God of providence explain all His ways and purposes to us before we will love and follow Him? As one poet wrote,

> *It is enough to know our sovereign God*
> *is on His throne above,*
> *It is enough to know our sovereign God*
> *rules oer our lives in love.*

3

Where Are the Clues in This Crime...?

Thou hast shown Thy people hard things....

The next few days were quite hectic, to say the least. We got little sleep as we tried to trace any potential lead. But there just weren't any! It was as if the driver and the car and Little Dinky had evaporated into thin air. The church set up an around-the-clock prayer schedule, and I spent a lot of my time at Dink and Janie's house.

Some days and even nights Dink and I would drive the roads beyond the point he had lost his grip and fallen from the car. In the daytime we would stop and ask people if they had seen the car or anything. We even knocked on hundreds of doors seeking someone who could tell us something. But nothing! I wondered how long Dink would insist on us doing this as all our efforts proved so futile. He kept saying, "We'se only needs one lead!"

The police did their best also, but they too found nothing. One could not manufacture leads as badly as one desired to do so. We were at a dead end---a stalemate which we found difficult to face. Each day began with new hope and a total obsession to find a clue, but then the day ended with discouragement and grief. Each day we prayed we would find something, but each day abandoned us to the oblivion of despair. As much as we prayed and as hard as we worked, there was not the slightest sliver or glimmer of encouragement.

The continual question which haunted Dink and Janie was that of "Why?" And when there was no answer given, their hearts sank into brooding and probing, even asking if God had abandoned them. I sought to answer them, but their sorrow seemed to destroy any energy they had to live or return to a normal life. And that truly was understandable. They seemed to be drifting into an abyss of greater hopelessness, and I actually feared they might come to the place where they would give up. I knew we had to do something, but what? I have never felt so helpless in all my life---yet, that is the way of tragedy and sorrow!

Then, finally, three weeks after the kidnapping a flame of faint hope surfaced, but it seemed like a candle burning in a hurricane. Dink's car was found about three hundred miles to the north. It had been ditched in a sleepy out-of-the-way lagoon which was about fifty feet deep. The police of that area called our local police department, and Troy talked to them and he passed the news on to me.

"Was anyone in the car?" I asked as he shared the news.

"No, not the driver nor Little Dinky," he replied.

"You're sure it was Dink's car?" I asked not sure whether I wanted a yes or no.

"No doubt about it!" he confirmed.

"Were there any fingerprints or other clues?" I searched further.

"Nothing!" he replied again with a sigh in his voice.

"So where do we go from here?" I asked.

"No where!" he said with discouragement. "We're right where we were three weeks ago when it happened."

It was my duty to share this information with Dink and Janie. I tried to do it without discouraging them, but they expressed little emotion as I shared the information---I couldn't hardly call it news.

The next day, though I felt it was hopeless except maybe as therapy for Dink and Janie, Dink and I drove the three hundred miles to the car. He went over the car with a fine-toothed comb, even though the police had already done the same. He figured he knew the vehicle better than anyone else, and that if something was different about it which might give a clue, he would find it.

Dink said nothing as he searched the car, until he got in under the steering wheel in the driver's seat. Then he looked up at me from the floor of the car, and for the first time in those three weeks, a faint smile emerged on his face.

"Preacha, it ain't much, but I can tell ya somtin' about da kidnapper!"

Who Are the Almandine...?

Fret not thyself....

I feared, as Dink smiled even a grim and wry smile, that he was grabbing at a straw which would lead no where. I wondered about the wisdom of renewing hope on the basis of such a slim thread-like lead---if there was one. Maybe Dink was losing it.

"Preacha, da kidnapper is a member of a national gang a criminals known as da 'Almandine.' Dey is named after a ancient city in Asia Minor, and da word refers to a violet variety of da ruby spinel or sapphire."

I blinked as he spoke, wondering if he was making it up or if it was really true.

He reached into his pocket and pulled out his key chain and held up a ring for me to see.

"Dis is da ring da members a dat gang wear. Do ya see dat sapphire, and do ya see da underside of da ring?" he asked.

I looked closely, and sure enough, it appeared to be a sapphire of some kind. And the underside of the ring part, which went around the inside of the finger, had a peculiar design---like a capital "A" on it.

"See dat 'A?'" Dink asked. "Dat's da Greek capital---da capital Alpha. It stands fer da 'Almandine' organization. An let me tell ya, deys da meanest gang alive! Ya has ta kill someone ta get inta dat gang!"

I gulped, wondering if that was why they kidnapped Little Dinky, and Dink must have read my mind.

"Nah, it ain't what you're tinkin---dey may be mean, but dey don't kill women and kids!" he sought to assure me.

"Then what would they want Little Dinky for?" I asked.

"Probly fer money. Dey sell da kids to some rich folks, sometimes even workin' through adoption agencies," he explained.

"Then Little Dinky is probably still alive!" I asked with some hesitation.

"You can bet on dat!" he said, almost with some joy to be assured he was alive.

"Dink, how do you know all of this!" I asked. "And how do you know the kidnapper was a member of that gang. Did you find his ring?" I asked, still somewhat puzzled.

"Come around da car, Preacha!" he instructed me.

He told me to get in on the floor of the passenger side of the front seat, and get on my back and look up at the underneath of the steering wheel. And sure enough, there it was---an "A" was impacted on the underneath side of the wheel---an "A" just like the one on the ring Dink had held up.

I still had some questions.

"How did that ring imprint get there so forcefully impacted in that manner?" I queried.

"Do ya remember dat I said I fought him while I hung onta da door jus' behind da driver? And dat he used his left hand to fight me off wid a knife? Dat means his right hand musta been grippin' dat steerin' wheel fer all it was worth, so dat he could control da car. An bein' a strong guy, wid a fierce grip, der it is---a clear 'A' on da wheel."

"But Dink, couldn't your ring have made that mark? You have a ring like his!"

"Nope! Impossible!" he stated very matter-of-factly. For the first time since the tragedy I saw the old Dink coming out. He was thinking and planning and organizing his next steps. He had hope!

"Well, why couldn't your ring have made that imprint?" I asked again.

"Cause I never wear my ring. I jus' keep it on my key chain," he explained.

Then another thought came to me.

"Dink, how did you get such a ring as that? You weren't a member of the Almandine, were you, before you got saved?"

"Preacha, der's a lotta tings you're probably better off not knowin'. Ya know I come from a gang background. Let's jus' leave it at dat."

I left it at that, but drew the assumptions. He had been a member of the Almandine, and if that were true he had gone through the initiation rite. I marveled again at the grace of God that had saved him and the change and growth since his salvation.

"What now?" I asked him.

"Let's go home. My heart's still heavy an broken, but Little Dinky's still alive, and I'se got some avenues ta seek ta trace him now."

I wondered if he meant he was going to resurrect some of his old Almandine contacts, but I rejoiced that I saw hope for the first time since the kidnapping.

On the way home he asked, "Preacha, does ya tink we can study sometin' in da word dat speaks 'bout God's providence in da next few months? I need it and Janie needs it. Whatta ya tink?"

Are the Almandine Ready for Us...?

Faith, mighty faith, the promise sees,
and looks to God alone....

Dink was very silent as we drove the three hundred miles back to Collegetown. I could tell he was thinking about the next move. When he had come to a conclusion, he spoke.

"Preacha, I'll tell ya what we'se gonna do!"

I didn't know if the "we'se" meant just Dink, or Dink and Janie, or if I was involved in these plans. If it had to do with the Almandine, I wasn't sure I wanted to be involved.

Dink continued.

"I'm goin right to da top!"

"To the top?" I repeated in the form of a question.

"Yes, sir. We'se goin ta New York---right to da top!"

He was close to the old Dink now. He was toying with me, disclosing information slowly, creating curiosity as he spoke.

"Dink!" I said firmly with a smile, "Explain yourself! Who is this 'we'se,' and what is in New York?"

"We'se is you and me, and New York is da contact point of da Almandine!" he offered.

"You and I are going to New York to visit this gang called the Almandine---the most violent and dangerous gang in the states?" I asked with a little fright in my voice.

"Yep! You and me ta New York tomorrow," he declared. "You will come wid me, won'tcha, Preacha? We can study da subject a providence as we travel, den I can pass it on to Janie."

"But New York? How do you know they will welcome you, and they surely would not welcome me!" I argued.

"Preacha, da Almandine has a sayin' dat dey live by. 'Once an Almandine, always an Almandine.' Dat means dey will receive me. Besides dat, what has been done is a violation of Almandine rules!" he declared with emphasis pounding his fist on the dashboard.

"Explain!" I urged again.

"It don't matter da rut'lessnes of da Almandine---dey has a rule never to commit no crime against a fellow Almandine member. Dat is da law of da organization. Da kidnappin' of Little Dinky has broke da rules of da Almandine, and when I informs dem of dat fact, we will get Little Dinky back---I guarantees ya."

"Okay, I do hope that is true. But won't they frown on you bringing me with you? I sure don't anticipate facing any member of the Almandine---unless he's been saved like you!" I protested.

"Oh, dat's covered too. Da Almandine has anudder rule. 'A true friend of one Almandine member is da true friend of all Almandine members.' Since you'se da closest friend I got, you are a friend of all Almandine members!" he explained.

I wasn't sure that thought was a comforting one or not. Then he explained further.

"Also, Preacha, da head man of da Almandine is an old close friend---I means a real old close friend. We came up tagether in da organization. If I hadn't got saved, I might be da head of da organization taday. He'll see us and be glad ta see us---I guarantees it. Wait and see."

"Dink, give me a day and I'll be ready to go. But let me ask a few more questions."

"Go ahead, Preacha, da floor is yours!" he said.

"Where do you think they have Little Dinky now? What happened after they kidnapped him? What will be the procedure to get him back?"

He explained that the kidnapping was rather routine as compared to others he had known. The kidnapper, after the kidnapping, would drive several hundred miles to a predetermined secluded and hidden place. There he would be met by another Almandine member. Together they would scuttle the car, and then take the child to one of a number of places. Then the child would be put up for adoption through a cooperating adoption agency, with all the paper-work being forged. Little Dinky by now was in his new home, or perhaps in a home or a pre-adoption place to seek to re-program his memory before adoption..

I asked him, "Don't you know where these places are, and couldn't we go straight to them?"

"Yeah!" he explained, "I knows where dey are (an ders more dan you tink), but dat ain't da way ya wants ta handle it. Whadda we gonna do, jus' walk in an kidnap him back?"

"Well, what about the old love of one Almandine for another? Couldn't you explain the mix-up and that they had stolen an Almandine's son?" I asked.

"Nah, dat ain't da way ta do it! Do ya tink da guy who made such a mistake would want ta be told about it by us? Or Little Dinky could be with some body who's not an Almandine member, who may not even know who da kidnapper was. Nope, we has ta go ta da top. Let dem trace him down fer us and bring him ta us, and deal wid whoever made da mistake. Dat's da way ta handle it!"

I must admit that I saw the wisdom of this approach. I had qualms about going anyway, and I surely didn't want to go at it the wrong way and mess with or confuse an Almandine member who might not play by the rules, especially if it meant our exposing his mistake.

We arrived home rather late, and decided to give ourselves a full day to get all things in order. The next day I cleared everything with the elders, lined one of them up to preach while we were gone, explained it all to Terry, my wife, and spent some time with Janie and Dink just to encourage them. She, like Dink, after he had explained it all, had a better spirit and greater hope, though I am sure she was like me, possessing some uncertainties about the whole thing.

I also grabbed my notes on providence and the book of Job, as I had been studying that very book (in God's providence) with the thought of preaching a series of sermons on it.

The next morning before dawn, we were off for the ten hour drive to New York. We took my car, since Dink's had not been replaced yet by the insurance company.

A quotation from George Mueller kept going through my mind:

> *Remember it is the very time*
> *For faith to work*
> *When sight ceases!*

This quote surely was true both physically and spiritually. I couldn't see the road ahead in the dark without our headlights, and I sure couldn't anticipate what we were to encounter when we faced the Almandine! God help us!

6

Who Rules the Affairs of This Universe..?

Behind a frowning providence, He hides a smiling face....

After about an hour of driving we stopped for breakfast, and Dink took over the driving chores. It was light by now, and I pulled out my Bible and read parts of Psalm 46:

1 God is our refuge and strength, a very present help in trouble. 2 Therefore will we not fear, though the earth be removed and though the mountains be carried into the midst of the sea; 3 Though the waters roar thereof and be troubled, though the mountains shake with the swelling thereof. Selah. 4 There is a river, the streams whereof shall make glad the city of God, the holy place of the tabernacles of the Most High. 5 God is in the midst of her; she shall not be moved. God shall help her, and that right early. 6 The heathen raged, the kingdoms were moved; he uttered his voice, the earth melted. 7 The Lord of hosts is with us; the God of Jacob is our refuge. Selah. 8 Come, behold the works of the Lord, what desolations he hath made in the earth. 9 He makes wars to cease unto the end of the earth; he breaks the bow, and cuts the spear in sunder; he burns the chariot in the fire. 10 Be still, and know that I am God; I will be exalted among the heathen, I will be exalted in the earth. 11 The Lord of hosts is with us; the God of Jacob is our refuge. Selah.

I took my outline of the passage and challenged our hearts with it.

I   THE PSALMIST HAD A COMMITMENT NOT TO BE AFRAID IN ANY CIRCUMSTANCE 2

    A. <u>The commitment</u> 2

       We will not fear....

       we will not be afraid
       we will not be filled with
           feelings of anxiety
           uncertainty of heart
           hopelessness

    B. <u>The circumstances</u> 2

       Though the earth be removed....
       Though the mountains be carried into the sea....
       Though the waters roar and are troubled....
       Though the mountains shake with swelling....

"Well, that just about covers everything!" I commented to Dink. "Though the earth disappears! Though the mountains fall into the sea! Though the waters roar against us as we are left with no land to grab onto. Though the mountains shake with trembling. Whew! We will not be afraid under any circumstance!!! Dink, I needed that---I don't know about you!" He nodded in agreement!

II THE PSALMIST HAD REASONS TO NOT BE AFRAID   1, 4-9

God is our refuge or hiding place!   1
God is our strength!   1
God is sovereign over the universe   4
   He is in His holy place   4
     in the city of God
     in the holy place
       of the tabernacle
       of the Most High
God is unmoved by the nations and their raging   6
   the nations raged and kingdoms were shaken
     but God uttered his voice
     and the earth melted
The Lord of hosts is with us   7
   the God of Jacob is our refuge
The Lord of hosts is in control of all things   8
   Come and behold the works of the Lord   8
     He makes desolations to cease in the earth   8
     He makes wars to cease to the end of the earth 9
     He breaks the bow and cuts the spear in sunder 9
     He burns the chariot in the fire 9

II THE PSALMIST HAD A COMMAND FROM GOD   10-11

Be still and know that I am God!   11
   I will be exalted among the nations
   I will be exalted in the earth
The Lord of hosts is with us   12
   The God of Jacob is our refuge

"How's that for encouragement for our trip?" I asked Dink. "God is our refuge and a very present help in trouble. Therefore we will not fear though the earth be removed, though the mountains be carried into the midst of the sea, though the waters roar and are troubled, though the mountains shake with the swelling thereof. God is in control---He is sovereign---He is providentially in control of all things. What should be our response to that, Dink?" I asked baiting him.

"All we need ta do is just sit down an shut up an keep still an let God be God! He's got everyting under control! We shouldn't complain, or try ta secon'-guess God, or speak words of complaint---jus' calmly and humbly submit ta Him. He's God! He receives His existence from nobody! He's governed by nobody! He's all-powerful, all wise, completely just an righteous! He's holy an infinitely good! He created everyting! He owns everyting! He's absolutely infinitely perfect in His bein' an all His ways! He seeks nobody's counsel! He needs nobody's counsel! He's thwarted by nobody, let alone a puny little man! His counsel is perfect! His counsel shall stand! He's aworkin everyting accordin' ta da pleasure of His own will! Hallelujah! Jus' sit down and shut up and know dat HE is God---not me, not you, not nobody but God!"

"Dink, do you know that you have just defined the doctrine of God's providence?" I asked.

"Yeah, I guess I did!" he said still praising the Lord.

I noted one theologian's definition of providence:

> God's works of providence are His most holy,
> wise, and powerful preserving and governing
> all his creatures and their actions.
> (Charles Hodge, Volume I, page 575)

"I guess the main problems that men have with God's sovereignty are that many, first of all, will not recognize that God is sovereign and providential over all things. Second, others admit in their doctrinal beliefs that God is sovereign and providential, but fight against it in their lives. We must be still and let God be God!" I challenged his and my heart also.

"Boy, dat sure does fit me dese last several weeks!" he admitted. "I didn't want ta let God be God when Little Dinky was kidnapped. I refused ta sit down an shut up an let God be in control of all tings. I fought Him, doubted Him, questioned Him, secon'guessed Him, and threatened ta quit Him. Forgive me, Lord!"

As he spoke he began to cry!

"But now, He's given us da victory! Lord, I submit ta You and Your will---whatever it is! Lord, we'se goin ta New York in Your name by Your power trustin' in You and Your will ta be worked out whatever it is. Lord, You is God, and Lord, I will not fear!!" he prayed.

I prayed after Dink, "Lord, my thoughts on Psalm 46 have given Dink the victory. Now Lord, give me the victory. Take away my fear of the Almandine! I will not fear whatever they do to us. Give me grace also to just sit down and shut up and let You be God. You're still on the throne working all things after the counsel of Your own will. Help me to remember that---whatever lies ahead!!!"

"Amen!!!" Dink and I both echoed, as we sped on to New York to meet the Almandine.

7

Is This within His Providence...?

Put thy trust in God, in duty's path go on....

We got to our hotel in New York (I have never seen such traffic in my life) about 6:00 in the evening. We were both very tired, and ready for bed, but Dink insisted on trying to contact his old friend in the Almandine that night. After we had checked into the hotel, and gotten a bite to eat, he boldly picked up the phone to call.

I have no idea what number he called, or who he expected would answer, but he was soon talking to someone in a whisper. The conversation didn't last very long, so as soon as he put the phone down, I began to question him.

"Who did you call?" I pressed him eagerly.

"I called a special number known only ta members of da Almandine," he replied.

"Who did you talk to?" I queried again. "Did you talk to your friend?"

"No, but I sent a message ta him sayin' dat I wanted ta see him immediately!" he answered.

I wasn't sure I liked that word immediately, and I was certain it was the wrong word when about forty-five minutes later there was a knock at our door, and two guys stood before me when I opened it.

"Are you the Dink!" one asked in a matter of fact tone of voice.

I didn't have a chance to answer, as Dink stepped forward and said boldly, "I'm da Dink! Who are you'se guys?"

They replied in some language I couldn't understand, and Dink answered them in similar words.

"Get yer tings, Preacha, cause we'se goin' wid dem!"

"What things should I get? You mean we don't get to sleep here tonight?" I asked somewhat puzzled.

"Get everyting! We'se checkin' out!" he explained.

"But what about the money we paid to stay here? New York isn't cheap, you know!" I argued.

"Don't worry, Preacha, we'll get our money back. De Almandine owns dis place," he assured me.

I thought to myself, "Lord, I need another dose of Psalm 46." Thus, I tried to remember the truths and commitment we had made that day as we drove to this place. I kept assuring myself that this is all in God's providence!

They helped us into a swanky limousine with shaded windows. I wouldn't have had any idea where I was going in a car with normal windows, since I had never been to New York. And with tinted windows, I didn't have a clue. Dink kept up a running conversation with the hoods in what must have been their secret language, so I didn't have a clue on that either. I just leaned back in the plush seat and sought to rest my weary body and mind.

After driving about an hour and a half or two hours, we turned into a long driveway going up to a country estate. I strained to see that much out the front window. They unloaded us into a room far fancier than the hotel room we had been staying in, and the hoods left.

"What's going on?" I asked Dink as soon as they left.

"We'se goin ta stay here tonight, I tink, and we'll see my friend tomorrow. Dis is da special room fer visitin' Almandine members. Snazzy ain't it!"

Snazzy wasn't the word!

"What time will your friend be here tomorrow?" I asked.

"Oh, dey said about 9:00 or so in da mornin'."

By that time it was 10:00 PM. and I asked Dink if he wanted to look into the Word of God before we went to bed. Normally, we might have considered ourselves too weary, but the reality of the events before us drove us to the Word.

I turned to my outlines of Job to lead us in our thinking:

I   THE CIRCUMSTANCES OF JOB BEFORE HIS TESTING WERE AWESOME BUT PROVIDENTIAL 1:1-11

I noted that
   he was an historical figure
   he lived in the land of Uz
   he lived probably during the days of the Patriarchs
   he knew the Lord---what a token of grace
   he worshipped the Lord
   he was careful before God
      for his own life
      for the lives of his children
   he was a godly man
      blameless
      upright
      shunned evil
   he had a wife and ten children
      seven sons and three daughters

he was extremely wealthy
the greatest of all men of the east
with 7000 sheep
with 3000 camels
with 500 yoke of oxen
with 500 donkeys
with a house full of servants
All of this was by the providential grace of God

II THE TESTING OF JOB WAS UNBELIEVABLE BUT PROVIDENTIAL 1:6-2:10

A. Job was accused by Satan before God 1:6-12

Satan came before God
he accuses Job of serving God
for what he can get out of God
he indicates
that Job isn't stupid
that he doesn't serve God for nothing
that God has hedged Job in
that Satan cannot touch him
that God has blessed Job
that Job is serving God and revering God
because of all the blessings
that God has given him
that if God were to remove the blessings
Job would curse God to His face
God allows the assault
Satan can take all his possessions
even his family
Satan cannot touch him
by sickness or by death

the question then is
> Will a man serve God because He is God?
> Or does a man serve God for the benefits?
> What will a man do when the blessings are gone?

B. Job loses all his possessions and his children but only within the providence of God   1:13-22

Within God's providence Job's property is taken
> the Sabeans took away his donkeys
> fire from heaven burns up the sheep
> the Chaldeans took away his camels
> but all of this is within God's providence
>> Satan could not have brought this upon him
>>> except within the providence of God
>> Satan had wanted to do this for a long time
>>> but now God allows it
>>> for it is part of His sovereign will
>> God is providential over secondary causes
>>> the fire from heaven
>>> the bands of men who come

Within God's providence Job's children are taken
> the number is ten

But through all of this Job is faithful
> which brings Satan to God again to complain
>> that Job serves only for the blessings
>> but if God were to take his health
>>> he would curse God to His face

C. Job loses his health but refuses to curse God   2:1-10

his body is filled with boils from head to foot
his wife rebukes him for not cursing God and dying

> his existence is on the garbage dump outside the city
> his accusing friends come to assail him

I stopped here to make a final point, knowing there was so much more that we could not cover this evening.

"Dink, if you had been Job, is there not something you would have done at this point?" I asked.

"Yeah, Preacha, da same ting I had been doin' fer three weeks. Askin' God why! Why God? Why God? Why God? I musta asked dat a million times even in my sleep."

"Is there anyone in Job's day who understood why?" I asked further.

"Nope! You're sure right der, Preacha. Nobody knew why---not his wife, not his friends, not even Job!!! His friends thought dey knew---but dey was wrong. I knows dat much about da book a Job."

"What does that teach us?" I asked for a final question for that night.

"That teaches dat when da trials an tragedies comes into our lives, dat we shouldn't ask God why, but that we should trust Him as our providential God, like in Psalm 46."

He thought awhile and continued.

"Dat means we shouldn't argue wid God, doubt God, accuse God, question God fer any a His dealins' wid us! We must bow to His providence, which I realize now ain't easy to do at times."

He paused a few moments in deep thought and then said, "Hey, Preacha, it seems ta me dat few Christians possess such a Biblical view of da providence a God."

About that time a knock came at our door---but only by the providence of God. Still I couldn't help but wonder, "What now, Lord? Am I submitted to your providence?"

Where Are We Going Now...?

My grace is sufficient for thee....

I let Dink answer the door, since he knew the language, and sure enough, they jabbered for a few seconds, and were gone.

"What's going on?" I asked as Dink closed the door.

"Grab your tings! We'se movin' agin." he replied.

"Where to and why?" I asked.

"I tink we'se goin' ta da bunker. Dat's where we'll meet da head man tomorrow. Don't get too excited, but I tink we'se der prisoners now!"

A few minutes later the hoods were back, and they led us out on the lawn in the darkness of the night to a helicopter. I had never ridden in one of those before, and not knowing where or what the bunker was, I must confess I had some concerns. And we were prisoners now?

However, I kept saying to myself, "I will not fear though the earth be cast into the sea! Be still and know that I am God. He is working all things after the counsel of His own will. All things work together for good to them that love the Lord and are called according to His purpose."

Then a thought came to me. Not only is it that we do not know where we are (maybe Dink does), but no one else does except these Almandine. In the hurry and scurry of the early evening I remembered that I hadn't even called Terry.

She had to be worrying about us, especially if she called the hotel where we were supposed to be staying.

Some phrases from a song went through my mind as we lifted from the ground. "Stayed upon Jehovah, hearts are fully blessed." Another part of that song said something about not a doubt of worry. And I told myself, that should be my attitude as I truly believed in the providential hand of my Father. No worry, no hurry, no scurry. No sweat, no fret, no regret---for those who trust His providence. I kind of played a mind game putting rhyming phrases together. No doubt, no pout. Some of my words were better than others.

As we got into the air and moved forward, I could see lights below and streams of traffic on highways, but I had no idea of any landmarks, so I still had not the faintest idea where we were.

I spoke to Dink and asked him if he knew where we were.

The only answer I got was, "Northeast a' New York City!" I thought to myself that could cover a lot of territory.

I found myself thinking of our next lesson in Job---his response to the providence of God. When the Lord took all his possessions and family, he said, "The Lord gave and the Lord has taken away. Blessed be the name of the Lord."

The text there in the early chapters of Job says that he worshipped God in this hour. I recognized that both of these statements, what he said and what he did, spoke of his submission to God, as horrible as the hour might have been. Surely his statement spoke of submission to God, even if he said it with a lump in his throat, a heaviness in his heart, and tears in his eyes. He bowed to the providence of God.

But then it also says he worshipped God, and that also speaks of submission to the providence of God. I asked myself what the heart of worship was? Not singing, not preaching, not any other of the accompaniments of worship, but the heart of worship is submission to God. Singing is not worship unless the heart is submitted to God. Preaching is not worship, unless there is submission to God. None of the other accompaniments of worship is the heart of worship. The heart of worship is submission.

Then I thought of Job's response to the second test, when he lost his health. His wife urged him to curse God and die. His response to her was that she was talking like a heathen woman. Didn't she know that both good and evil come from God's hand? Again he evidences that he was submitting to the providence of God in his life, even if he did not understand what God was doing.

I noted in my mind, for my own edification and comfort, that Job's response to his easy providence (when he had everything) was submission. His response to his difficult providence (when his possessions and family were taken) was submission. His response to his impossible providence (when his health was taken) was submission also.

I began to pray that the Lord would give to Dink and me submissive hearts---especially me. Dink had run with these kind of guys in his pre-conversion day, and probably had more understanding of what they were doing and why they were doing it. But to be honest, I was scared half to death---until the Lord strengthened me by His Word.

We started to descend, but I couldn't make out our landing area. "What's next?" I asked Dink.

"You'll see! Maybe da big boss!"

"Here? At this hour---2:00 o'clock in the morning?"

"Yep, if dats God's will!" he reminded me with a smile.

How Can I Get My Son Back...?

Afflictions cannot injure, when blended with submission....

As we settled down to earth, I wanted to ask Dink if he had been here before. But I decided against that when the area was suddenly overrun by more hoods---with guns!

It was another remote area (no house), and I had not seen any lights of other houses or estates as we came in to land. Then all of a sudden a door opened in a mound before us which had looked like a grassy hill, and we entered another very swanky place. I hadn't seen any buildings on top of the ground, so I concluded that this was all hidden from above for security purposes.

They led us into a room that had one light focused on a desk with a fancy chair and a man in it. The man was dressed in black, had a pock-marked face with a cigar stuck in his mouth, and he had a swept-back hairdo with enough oil to make his hair glisten in the light shining on him and the desk.

When he saw us, he got to his feet, dismissed all the body guards, and a welcome smile came to his face, for which I was grateful. He stuck his hand out to Dink, and spoke in a husky voice.

"Hey, its good to see the Dinker!" he said with a small laugh under his breath.

"Yeh, its good ta see ya too, Frankie!" Dink replied. "How've ya been?"

"Oh, I'm fine!" he said, and then he began to cough.

"Whatsamatta, Frankie. Ya don't sound too good ta me?"

"Well, I got a little cold. Not enough to worry about! But that's the Dink. He always had too much compassion for others!" he stated with another heavier laugh, which again was followed by deep coughing.

"Frankie, let me introduce ya ta someone!" Dink offered. "Dis is my preacha, Pastor Ira Pointer."

"Yeah, I know who he is. He did something I thought no one could ever do. He's the guy that got you out of the Almandine! Maybe we ought to kill him!" Frankie said with another laugh. "But, hey, a true friend of an Almandine is a friend of every Almandine. I'm glad to meet you, preacher. No hard feelings---but you robbed the Almandine of its future head---maybe even before me or at least next after me!"

"Well, let me tell ya sometin,' Frankie! No preacha got me outa da Almandine. Only da Lord Jesus Christ coulda done dat."

With which Dink witnessed to Frankie for about ten minutes. I must admit I had some mixed emotions about that, but that was the Dink. He was bold to witness to anyone at any time. That took precedence over anything--- even his own concerns. I wondered what would happen if Frankie would get offended or upset at our witness, but that didn't seem to bother Dink, and rightfully so.

I could tell as the conversation continued that Frankie was moved. I felt like I was in the presence of the apostle Paul as he witnessed to Agrippa. Dink pressed him as Paul pressed Agrippa, and even asked a similar question.

"Frankie, do ya believe dese things? Do ya believe dat Jesus Christ is God and dat He came ta earth and took da form of a man ta die on da cross ta pay da penalty of da sins of all who trust Him?" He had already pointed out his sin!

"Dink, let me tell you something no one else knows," he continued in his husky voice, which I began to see as perhaps part of a health problem. "I trust you with this information because you are the only true friend I have had in years. You know the Almandine talk about friends, but that is not true. You are a friend of the Almandine only as long as you do their bidding. If you ever leave them, the friendship stops. I don't think anyone else, except me, would have seen you, even though you were an Almandine, because you turned your back on the organization."

"Yeah, I knows dat, Frankie. I was dependin' on you ta see me an help me. I probly wouldn't a tried if da leader was some body else."

"Let me quickly tell you two things, Dink. First, I am dying of cancer. I don't know how long I will be alive. If circumstances were different, I could very easily become a Christian. But I'm in too deep with the Almandine. Right now they are my protection and insurance. As long as I am alive, I am assured of the best treatment and highest respect. If I believed in this Jesus Christ as you did (and you are a strong persuader of my need---I recognize that), then all of my present comforts would cease. I would have no power or authority, and no care for these dying days which I have already entered. Do you understand what I am saying."

"Yeah, Frankie, I understands! You're sellin' out yer soul an eternity with da Lord Jesus Christ in heaven fer a few crummy days a comfort and importance on earth. Dat sounds like a poor bargain ta me. I thought you was a better business man dan dat!" Dink declared boldly.

I was glad to hear Dink challenge him, but I hoped he didn't press the matter too far for Little Dinky's sake. But as it unfolded, I realized that Dink knew Frankie well, and it seemed that boldness was part of their previous relationship, as well as part of existence in the gang world.

"Dink, you're right! I guess it is a bad deal. I wish I could believe in this matter about eternity and salvation through Christ as strong as you do. I will think about it!" he promised as he looked pensively into the darkness of the room beyond him, losing, it seemed, even the consciousness of our presence for a few moments.

"Frankie, you said der was two tings you wanted ta tell me. Da first was yer sickness. What's da odder one?"

"Oh, yes! Dink, I know why you are here!"

"Ya do?" Dink asked with surprise.

"Yes, you are here about the kidnapping of your son by the Almandine."

"Den you admit dat it was da Almandine?" Dink asked as he sensed he was hot on the trail now.

"Yes it was the Almandine!" Frankie admitted.

"Well, den you'll help me get him back, won't ya?" Dink almost demanded.

"It's not that easy, Dink!" he protested.

"Whaddaya mean, it ain't dat easy! Is you da big man or not?" Dink pressed now with a challenge.

"Well, you don't understand!" Frankie protested.

"Well, den tell me so's I can understand!" Dink countered with fire in his eyes. "Dey took my son! Dat is against da Almandine rules. You knows dat! None of da crimes or work of da Almandine is to be perpetrated against an Almandine member! Am I right or wrong? Tell me!"

"Well, Dink, that is a general rule for all Almandine members. But you complicated it when you got religion and left the organization. The council for the following years looked for ways to get even with you or get you back.

The kidnapping was on purpose. We just didn't make a mistake. It was planned!"

"Well, den unplan it!" Dink demanded.

"I would if I could, Dink. But this is out of my hands now." Frankie pled.

"Whaddaya mean, outa yer hands. You'se is da big man, aintcha? Or has da Almandine come ta where its run by a council!" Dink challenged again.

"Well, I'm afraid changes are taking place. Do you realize how difficult it is to maintain supreme authority over a mob like this? Its not like it was in the old days, Dink," he stated with some fear in his eyes.

"And my sickness seems to weaken my authority as well. It seems the vultures have already started to gather to devour my flesh when I die, and to take over as the supreme leader," he tried to explain.

"So what's da bottom line! Is ya tellin' me der's no hope to get Little Dinky back?" Dink said almost assailing him. I must admit, I felt sorry for Frankie. He was sick. He was dying. He was weakened in his leadership. He understood the gospel and admitted that he needed Christ. He was now caught in the middle of a power struggle that would determine the future of the son of an old friend and associate---maybe the only true friend he had ever known.

"The bottom line is this, Dink. The only way you can get your son back is for you to return to the Almandine and reject this religious profession you have made. Then and only then will you get your son back. I will give you four days to think about it, and then you must give an answer!"

10

You Want to Break Out of Here...?

No bliss I seek, but to fulfill,
In life, in death, Thy lovely will....

As the meeting with Frankie closed, Dink still had fire in his eyes and heart. We were told that we would be detained there for four days, and Frankie would return for Dink's answer. Dink tried to tell him there was no reason to wait, because he would never sell out his Savior. But Frankie insisted that we be detained, and for Dink to think about it before giving a final answer. With that he left.

In a few moments the hoods came back in and escorted us to a room further back in the bunker. We were told this would be our residence for the next four days, and if we needed anything, to push a certain button. We were shown two large swanky rooms, along with two separate bathrooms---a room for each of us. Then the door closed and we heard a click which indicated we were being locked in. We checked the door, and sure enough, that was the case.

I immediately pressed the button, for one thing, to see if it worked. And immediately two well-armed hoods were there. I asked them if we could contact our families, and we were informed that they had already taken care of that. We had to take their word for it, and I hoped it was true, but there was no way to be certain.

By now it was about 5:00 in the morning, and we hadn't had any sleep all night, so after prayer we crashed in the plush beds to try to give our bodies some relief from a very long day. I told Dink to wake me when he woke up, and he promised he would, and I agreed to do the same for him---that is, if it was past noon. I figured we needed at least that much time for sleep.

I found it strange waking up in a room without any windows because of being in a bunker. But as I glanced at my watch, I noticed it was about 10:30 A.M. I dozed and rested a little longer, and finally got up about 11:30, but noticed that Dink was up already.

"How did it go last night?" I asked him.

"Not well!" he replied. "I've been awake since 'bout 9:30. Just couldn't sleep!"

And then he stated the question on both of our hearts, as he asked, "Preacha, is all dis parta God's providence?"

I didn't know exactly how to tell him it was, so I queried if I could ask him a question or two. He agreed.

"If God is not in control of this, that is providential over it, who is? You or me? The Almandine? Somebody else on earth? The devil? Or is it just chance?"

"You'se got me der. God has ta be in control. If we was ta conclude dat He's not, den we no longer got da God who's revealed in da Bible! And den where does we turn ta find out who's in control?"

I went back over what we had seen in Job, to be sure we had covered it all together, and I mentioned the material I had used to encourage my heart as we had traveled. I then pressed the button, and asked for some food, and we settled into our day as we began with a study of the Bible. What else did we have to do besides study and pray?

I thought it might be helpful to begin a discussion about the hopeless situation that Job faced in the next section of our study. Following his loss of his possessions, his children and his health, he became an outcast. That means he was ostracized by his friends, family and business associates. He now has boils all over his body, from the top of his head to the bottom of his feet. Some think this was leprosy. Whatever the case, his body is full of scabs which itch fiercely, so that he must take a piece of old broken pottery and scrape the itching which afflicted him.

Plus, he must go live outside the city on the garbage dump, where the refuse is burned daily. Here the dogs come to gnaw at the garbage and the bodies which have died. Here he lives without much shelter. His bedroom is his bathroom (and everybody else's) and his bathroom is his bedroom. Here he lives when the cold chills his body, and when the heat is fierce and overwhelming. Here and under these conditions he seeks sleep, but how often it flees from him because of the horrible circumstances, including the pain in his body. Here he scavenges for food from among the garbage.

It must have been quite a shocking experience for Job to come to the realization that this was the only place he could go. Here is a man who had been welcomed at kings' banquets, and associates' business gatherings, and family festivals. Now no one welcomes him---not his family, not his friends, and not his business associates. He has nothing to offer them, except the shame and stench of his diseased stinking body. He has no hopes of ever recovering to be anything close to what he had been previously, so men would not even help him with an eye toward the future.

Thus Job was left entirely alone in the world, with no hope or encouragement for today or tomorrow. He seemed to be forsaken by God also. Remember that he was not aware of the conversation in heaven between God and Satan, the enemy of God and all mankind.

"I guess we'se got it pretty good comparin' ta Job!" Dink observed.

"Yes, and remember something else. He had no Bible to encourage him, no fellowship with other believers, no promises of God stated in propositional form, no biographies of great Christians, no theology books to read to define providence for him, no sermons hidden in his mind, no Christian songs to sing, no poetry to recite, no Savior who had died, no Gethsemane, no Calvary, no Christ as His great high priest, and on and on we could go!" I explained.

"Yeah, I guess he was sometin' of a pioneer fer us. He was pioneering through dat dark wilderness of pain an sorrow, blazin' a trail in sufferin', so da pathway could be easier fer us!" Dink explained.

About that time the food arrived. One hood brought it into us, while the other one kept a gun trained on us. We prayed after they had left, and then did enjoy the meal as best we could under such circumstances.

Then Dink shook me up, when he said, "Hey, Preacha, we's gonna get outta here! Are ya wid me?"

11

How Could I Have Spoken This Way...?

Untested faith is merely carnal confidence....

Any plans for an immediate escape ended quickly as another knock came at our door. When I invited whoever it was to come in (they controlled the lock), the door opened and we received the shock of our lives!! There standing between the two hoods was Little Dinky!! Dink jumped from the chair and bounded to the door before anything could be said. Then one hood spoke.

"The boss said you could see him every day. He said something about it might help you make up your mind."

I feared that Dink might try to overpower the guards now---regardless of the guns. But he swept Little Dinky off his feet and hurried him inside the room. Little Dinky was glad to see his daddy, but I could tell he was confused. He clung to his father like he would never let go.

The hoods left him with us most of the afternoon, but then whisked him away about 5:00 P.M. I thought Dink was going to war to prevent that, but he finally gave in---but not without much crying and many tears from all of us, including Little Dinky. After all he was only two years old.

Then Dink broke down! He began to question the providence of God.

"Preacha, how can all of dis be in His providence? If it is, it wouldda been better if Little Dinky had never been born, and maybe just as well if I'd never been born either!

How can God allow someone ta have ta go through all of dis?"

I could tell that he was at the bottom of the world!

He cried with heavy and heaving sobs over his son and his helplessness to rescue him.

"Maybe I do need to renounce....," he began, but he never ended the sentence.

I thought of the cruelty of the Almandine and even Frankie in all of this, and, I must admit, that my sympathy for Frankie in his condition plummeted. I concluded that these guys weren't playing any games---they were ruthless and would stop at nothing, if they had planned all of this. The Lord and submission to his will was our only hope of survival and even maintaining our sanity.

I explained all of this to Dink, and the Lord used it to help him get control of himself once again, as his faith returned.

Then still crying he said, "Preacha, even though I might say it, I could never do it---renounce Jesus, dat is. He's my Lord, an I hasta walk in submission ta him. Jesus an da Father didn't sell me out when da goin' got rough. Jesus went all da way to da cross in da most horrible death ta save an old wretch like me, and da Father not only watched it, but He had willed it from eternity past. He gave His son ta save me."

Then he stopped speaking to me and spoke to God as he said, "And Father, I give my son ta ya now. I don't know what You're doin' but You do, an dat's good enough fer me. I don't hasta know as long as You know and its in Your will. Lord, guide us ta do what's right now, and not jus' what our human emotions want."

I knew now he had the victory, and whenever they might bring Little Dinky back, he was ready, even though tears still might come at each meeting and each parting.

Then he began to apologize.

"Preacha, I'm sorry I broke down. I ain't very strong in da Lord. I only been saved a few years, ya know."

That opened the door for me to explain to him how Job broke down under his seemingly-impossible circumstances, when his friends came to visit him.

He even cursed the day he had been born (chapter 3).

He also asked why he had not died at birth, and why he could not even now find peace in the grave, when he was willing and desirous of death.

He said he sought death as a man searched for hidden treasures, but he could not find it.

He questioned God for letting him live under such conditions.

I then explained how we should not condemn or criticize Job, but seek to understand him.

His sorrow pressed him beyond his ability to reason and understand, something we seem always to demand so we can stay in control of a situation.

His heart may have resolved a thousand times not to break under the weight of his circumstances, but he was crushed beyond his human ability to keep his previously bridled tongue silent.

His sores hounded and tormented him through endless days and sleepless nights, till his heart exploded and had to erupt to send forth pitiful moans and questions before his God.

His unending pain was like a raging, swelling river which beat against the dike which held it, until the dam finally broke, to send forth devastation and destruction as his mind near insanity and his body near the breaking point of unendurable suffering had to vent itself through his speech.

But even at that, Job never cursed God.

He only asked for an explanation or death, which God never gave him.

He had forgotten the many blessings of the past years in light of his present trials.

He had concluded that there was no way through his wilderness trials, and he would never emerge from his darkness.

He was judging life by the quality of his life---which at this point seemed very low to him. What purpose was he serving? What hope was there for the future? He had surrendered the truth for his own human reason, and when human reason collapsed, so did his faith and hope.

He had come to the place where he no longer rested in the providence of God, but like so many today, he began to ask questions which God is not obligated to answer, and in many cases doesn't answer---all the why questions (Why did God allow this to happen? Why didn't God stop this from happening? Why is there pain and suffering in this world?)

These are questions which can never be solved, yet multitudes refuse to accept this as an answer. Men demand to know! Men say they will refuse to believe and trust God until they do understand. Men turn bitter as they face the afflictions of life, but find no answers, except the answer that it is enough for God to be God.

"Tanks, Preacha. Tanks fer showin' me dat ya understands and God understands our frailties," he spoke with a renewed faith.

By now it was about 7:30 P.M. We called for some food, and then retired early, as we were still pretty worn out from the previous day's experiences and the present day's emotional pain.

As I drifted off to sleep this night I wondered about many things, but especially I asked how this all was going to end. I knew Dink was not going to renounce Christ. Therefore, it was up to the Almandine from a human standpoint. But God was in control over it all, regardless of what the Almandine did or did not do.

I also recalled some of the words of one of my favorite preachers:

> *Remember that we have no more faith*
> *at any time than we have in the hour of trial.*
> *All that will not bear to be tested*
> *is mere carnal confidence.*
> *Fair-weather faith is no faith at all.*
> *C. H. Spurgeon*

12

Is This a Trial of Extraordinary Grace...?

Patient perseverance springs out of suffering....

The second day of Dink's time to consider the future of his son began rather calmly. No one disturbed us till about ten o'clock the next morning. They had brought breakfast at our request, but now they came knocking on the door. They told Dink there was someone who wanted to see him, but that I couldn't go with him. So he left, and I was alone wondering, but also praying, for whatever it was that he was facing.

About an hour and a half later they brought him back. I didn't have to ask him what had taken place, as he began to bubble the moment he got into the room.

"Preacha, does ya know what dey did ta try ta break me dis time?" he burst forth as soon as the door closed.

"I have no idea, Dink. You will have to tell me!" I replied, thinking to myself that this was no time to play his usual word games.

"Preacha, dey had some philosopher kinda preacha in dat room where we met wid Frankie! He tried ta talk or reason me inta renouncin' Jesus!" he explained.

"What did he say? Did he argue with you from the Bible?" I asked.

Then he unfolded the conversation which had taken place between them, and I concluded that this "preacha" (whoever he was) must have thought he had a tiger by the tail. I venture to say he had never met someone like "da Dink."

Dink told me that they took him into this room, introduced this guy to him, and then left them alone. This "preacha" began to give Dink arguments against the Christian faith. The Bible is not true! Jesus Christ is not God! Christ never rose from the grave. There is no heaven or hell---we all make our own hell on earth.

About this time Dink asked him how he knew all these things? What was his authority to believe what he believed and to reject what he rejected in the Christian faith? He said that some of these things he had learned by experience. Dink asked him if he had been there when Jesus didn't rise from the dead. He stuttered and answered, "Well, no.!" Dink told him then that his experience wasn't much good to settle the resurrection.

Dink then asked him how he had concluded that Christ is not God? Had God told him that? He said no, but that such an idea was against his human reason. Dink asked him how he could depend so certainly on his reason---was he the smartest man in the world, or better yet was he omniscient knowing everything there was to know about everything? He admitted that he was not the smartest man in the world and he certainly did not know everything. Dink told him it didn't look like his human reason was any more dependable for knowing the truth than his experience.

By now this "preacha" was getting a little frustrated with Dink, but Dink didn't let up. He asked him how he knew the Bible was not true. The "preacha" answered that it had errors in it. Dink asked him to name one. He couldn't at first, and then he said the Bible had geographical errors. Dink asked him to name one of those, and he just stuttered and stammered. Dink asked him next if those supposed errors he was talking about (though he couldn't name any) were problems of textual variants, which would make the discussion a whole different subject. He didn't know what a textual variant was.

He then told Dink he was a fool to ignore the great scholars of the past. He challenged Dink to read them and they would inform him of the errors of the Bible. Then Dink unloaded on him. Dink said that he didn't care if men called him a fool, that was nothing. The fool is not the man who believes the Bible, but the fool is the one who denies the Bible. Then he quoted the verse in Luke where Jesus called the disciples on the road to Emmaus fools because they were slow of heart to believe all that the Old Testament prophets had written.

Dink also pointed to the verses in I Corinthians where Paul says the wisdom of God is foolishness to men, but the wisdom of man is foolishness to God. Thus man's wisdom is the real foolishness. Therefore he told this "preacha" he was the real fool.

I guess that ended their conversation, because Dink could only shake his head and exclaim, "Talk about a fool---dat guy was it. But I made him set der while I gave him da gospel."

And that did end their discussion. The "preacha" called for the guards and told them Dink was a hopeless case, and immediately left.

"What does ya tink of dat, Preacha?" he asked me as he closed the story.

"Well, that sounds a lot like the book of Job in chapters 3-7," I explained. "Job's friends have come to 'comfort' him, but end up assailing him. Eliphaz in these chapters tells Job that he is in the condition of all this suffering because he is a very sinful man. If he will only confess his sin and get

God's forgiveness, he will be restored to all the blessings. He told Job he could be assured of all of this because God had revealed it to him in a dream."

"What'd Job tell him?" Dink asked with great interest.

"Well before Job spoke, Eliphaz told Job he needed to go read the great wise scholars of the past!" I explained.

"Well, what's Job say to dat?" he asked eagerly again.

"Finally, Job responded in chapter 6. He told Eliphaz of the greatness of his misery. It was greater than the sands of the sea. It was from the Almighty. It is not just the imagination of Job's mind. It is so great that Job wishes he could die. It is so great that he is fearful he might deny God."

"Wow, dat rings a bell, don't it---especially since dey asked me to deny the Lord to save Little Dinky!" he said very soberly.

"Job says further that his misery is so great that he has no hope, yea, not even any friends!" I added.

"Wow, dat was a smasher to dose good old boy so-called buddies, too, wasn't it?" he declared.

"Dink, there are a lot of lessons here for us," I stated. "Even some of the lessons you have learned today."

"Yeah, Preacha, you're right!" he said as if the light bulb of truth had surged brighter in his mind.

Then we began to list the lessons:

1. Theological truth is important---false theology is dangerous.

2. Theological truth is based on the Word of God--- it cannot be built on the feeble reason of man. Human reason sounds convincing and logical, at times, but the truth of God possesses mysteries

which the human mind cannot understand. Thus theology which brings us the truth cannot be based on experience or human reason. It must be based on the revelation of God to us---which for us today is the Bible.

3. Theological truth must be given to others. If it is the truth which sets man free, and if God has revealed that truth to us, then we must share it with others. Truth was never meant for just the private consumption of believers. We must give it to others.

4. Theological truth must be ministered to others with compassion. Be careful of ministering the truth to others with a cold callused heart, like Eliphaz did to Job. (At this point Dink checked his heart as he had spoken to "da preacha").

5. Theological truth when ministered to others must be accompanied by humility. Beware of giving forth the truth in pride and arrogance. (Again, Dink checked his heart).

6. Theological truth when ministered to others must be applied correctly. Beware of some who have the truth but twist it in applying it to others and even to themselves

7. Theological truth will never claim to solve all the mysteries of God. That was the trouble with these friends of Job. They possessed what we might call a "vending machine" view of the justice of God. If

you put godliness into the machine of God's divine justice, you will get out continual blessings. If one puts in an ungodly life, he will automatically bring immediately to his own life sufferings and afflictions. There are no exceptions. There is absolutely no other possibility. There is no argument over this point, according to Job's friends. The truth is that there are mysteries in God's providence. The godly do suffer at times, and the ungodly do prosper. Beware of any one who claims to have solved all the divine mysteries of God.

8. Theological truth will never limit the providence of God. Beware of anyone who wants to limit God's providence in favor of the power of man. It is not that God is providential, but.....! It is not that God rules over all things, but.....! It is not that God's providence covers all things, but.....! It is that God by His providence is ruling all things....period!

After we had discussed all of this for a little longer with rejoicing hearts, Dink said, "Preacha, ain't it great how da Lord encourages da hearts of His servants wid da truth, even as we'se in da middle of dis trial?"

We prayed, and then ordered some lunch, and stretched out on the beds for a nap.

I could hear Dink singing and praying in his room. It was clear that he had come to see and understand the truth as spoken earlier by a man of God of history. He had said:

Extraordinary afflictions are not always the punishment for extraordinary sins, but sometimes the trial of extraordinary grace.

13

What Have They Done to Dink...?

Hitherto hath the Lord helped us....!

On this second day of our captivity (I hoped that it would only last for the promised four days), we were awakened from our naps about 5:00 in the afternoon. This time the knock at the door brought the request that I go with them, while Dink stayed in the room.

Again, they led me into the same room where we had met Frankie and where Dink had been interrogated. Sitting behind the desk was either the same "preacha" or another one. He now wanted to try to "talk some sense into my head so I could talk some sense into that idiot Dink's head," as he put it in his opening statement. He was a more modern kind of preacher in his dress and in his speech.

"Look man!" he said as he tried to reason with me. "Don't you know that the Almandine have power over you, your friend Dink, and his kid? Don't you think you had better help him to see that the only way he can save that kid is to renounce his Christian faith and rejoin the Almandine."

I replied, trying not to sound like a smart aleck, with the method of Jesus when he was before Pilate.

"Sir, don't you know that you have no power over me or Dink or Little Dinky except God allows you? I would be careful if I were you to be involved in what the Almandine have done and are further threatening to do. You will never be able to flee from the God of heaven for your sins. You may prolong the judgment for a while. You may not face your judgment until you are in eternity, but then it will be for eternity that you will be punished for your actions!"

He tried to act like my words didn't phase him, but I could tell he was shook as he attempted to speak again.

"Don't tell me you believe in that hell-fire and damnation kind of preaching. You look like a lot more educated and bright young man than that?" he tried to say with confidence.

"Sir, I believe the Bible. And if you want to talk about brilliance and brightness, it seems to me that its a pretty dull mind that gets tangled up the Almandine. How can you justify kidnapping and murder and extortion and all the Almandine stand for? Talk about stupid---how did you get mixed up with this bunch? Not because you were smart. I'll bet you've wished a dozen times that you had never started this road of association with them. The reality is, if you would only admit it, that you are the captive of the Almandine, not us. We are free in Christ, you are bound in sin. We are free within His power to protect and preserve us, while you are a slave to their bidding. Talk about stupid! Talk about talking sense into someone's head---you need it far more than we do. Why don't you let us help you? That's the only real way you can help us as well as yourself. Let us help you!"

It seems he gave up on me sooner than he had Dink. Because with several curse words he called the hoods, and they took me back to our rooms. I kept my eyes open on the way back, hoping to learn something. Maybe Little Dinky was still there.

When I got back to the room, Dink was gone, so I sat down and read my notes on Job so I could share them later with Dink. We were up to chapter 8 by now.

That's the chapter where Job's second friend speaks. He rebukes Job for his supposed irreverent speech and his improper theology. He argues the righteousness and justice of God. He challenges Job to look to God and plead with Him, if he is pure and upright. He says that if he does that, then God will rouse Himself on Job's behalf even now and restore him to his rightful place. Job will be even more prosperous than before.

He also rebukes Job for his supposed ignorance of the wisdom of the fathers. He challenges Job to realize he was only born yesterday and to learn from the fathers of the former generations. He tells Job what the fathers taught:

1. God works according to laws   8:11-12
2. God's law for men is clear--the godless perish   8:13
3. The godless perish
   because their faith is false 8:14-15
   because they are not rooted in God   8:l6-19
4. In simple words to apply this to Job
   Job is not blameless before God
   Job needs to get right with God
   Job will then be blessed again

I made some further notes for sharing this material with Dink:

1. Bildad had correct foundational principles for theology:
   God is righteous and just
   God will not pervert justice
   God will do what is right
   God will not do what is wrong

2. Bildad's problem in building his theology was that he misapplied his foundational principles as he concluded the following from the above principles:

    a. All suffering which comes into a man's life is because of sin

    b. All sin is punished immediately in this life

    c. All suffering because of sin will be removed immediately if a man repents and changes and turns his life toward godliness

    d. All suffering will continue until a man repents, therefore immediate repentance is a necessity

    e. All the suffering from sin will be removed and man will be returned to prosperity and health when he repents

I noted in writing that even though Bildad had two correct foundational principles (that God is righteous and is working according to His laws), his conclusions and application from them (as stated just above) were incorrect. I noted also several other truths from which men have drawn false conclusions (the "if" clause is true, but the conclusion drawn from it is not):

1. If God is a good God, then He cannot be the creator of such a world that is so full of sin

2. If God is a good God and did create the world, then He is a powerless God in light of the sin in the world

3. If God is a God of providence (ruling over all things),
    then man cannot have a will that acts freely (freely
    in the sense of unforced by God)

4. If man is a creature that acts not forced by God, then
    God cannot be a God of sovereignty and providence,
    ruling over all things

5. If God is a God of providence, then man is no more than
    a robot

6. If the Trinity is true, then we have more than one God

7. If God is one God, then the Trinity cannot be true

8. If God is a God of love, then there cannot be a hell

9. If God is a God of love, then all men will be saved

10. If the Bible is written by men, then it must have errors
    in it

11. If salvation is by grace, then men are free to live any
    way they please after they are saved

12. If salvation is by grace, then Christians do not have to
    be concerned to live a holy life

13. If works have no place in salvation, then there was no
    purpose for God to give the law

14. If Jesus is God, then He cannot be a man

15. If Jesus is a man, then He cannot be God

16. If God has a people who He has elected to salvation, then evangelism and missions are unnecessary

17. If God has foreordained all things that come to pass, then there is no reason for us to pray

18. If the righteous suffer along with the unrighteous, then there is no good reason to serve the Lord

19. If the unrighteous often prosper more than the believer, then there is no reason to be a believer

20 If human reason is faulty in doing theology, then our theology will be irrational and worthless

Again I noted that part of the problem was our failure to allow for any mysteries in our faith. Human reason had to reign supreme in doing theology. Anything that would not pass the bar of human reason, had to be thrown out of one's theological system.

I listed truths to remember about human reason:

1. Human reason is not supreme

2. Human reason is not free from the effects of the fall

3. Human reason must be regenerated to be able to think God's thoughts

4. Human reason must be under the authority of the Word of God

5. Human reason must be under the guidance of the Holy Spirit

6. Human reason when not under the Word guided by the Holy Spirit
    thinks it is brilliant and capable
    thinks it is supreme
    thinks it has no limits
    thinks it does not need God
    thinks it does not need regeneration
    thinks it does not need the Word of God
    thinks it does not need the Holy Spirit
    therefore it draws all kinds of false conclusions
        as it constructs a God and theology
        that is fully understandable
            to its own categories of thought
            to its own whims of emotion
            to its own likes and desires
    therefore it stumbles all over the place
        rejecting clear truths in the Bible
        drawing conclusions negated in the Bible

About the time I was finishing these thoughts, Dink was returned to the room. He came in propped up between the two hoods. He was all beat up and black and blue, but he was proclaiming victory as he said, "Preacha, hitherto hath da Lord helped us...!"

Then he slumped to the floor as he passed out.

I was left alone as the hoods slammed the door.

They seemed to be getting mad now!

I began to wonder if we would ever get out of this place alive!!

14

Is This Part of God's Providence...?

When I am afraid, I will trust in Thee....!

I revived Dink by splashing some water on his face, and then helped him to the bed. He was groggy but was still rejoicing.

"Praise da Lord, Preacha. Da Lord sustained me! I been beat up by better hoods dan dat! An I gots in some good blows also!"

I encouraged him to lean back on the pillow and rest, which he did for about ten minutes. But it was clear that though his eyes were closed, his mind was still going ninety miles a hour.

"Preacha, we'se gotta get outa dis place---an soon!" he mumbled.

I admitted to him that I had entertained the same thought, but I wondered why he had come to that conclusion.

"Dey is gettin serious now. I don't know what's wrong wid Frankie. Dis seems ta be outa his control. I don't tink Little Dinky is still here, so why should we stay? Dese guys is unpredictable!" he explained.

"What makes you think Little Dinky is not here?" I asked him.

"Jus' my experience wid the Almandine! But we'll make sure of dat before we leave dis place!" he added.

"But these doors are locked!" I protested, not a protest to stay, but a protest for information.

"Wait till da middle of da night! I'll get us outa here!" he proclaimed.

With that he dropped off to sleep, and I wondered if he would feel the same way when he woke up. I stretched out on my bed, not knowing when Dink would wake up and want to try to break out of our swanky prison. I figured I might need some rest also. As I tried to snooze, I couldn't help but think about Dink and what I knew about him.

I did know that he had grown up in the midwest around the St. Louis area. His father had been a brick contractor, and Dink had started off at a young age helping him by carrying bricks and blocks at the construction sites. This explained his enormous strength for a guy who was just five feet eight inches tall (so he claimed). He didn't have to lift weights, because he lifted blocks every day.

I also knew that he had been a rough character in high school, and something of an athlete. He had played football, even nose tackle on defense, because of his tremendous strength. This strength must have given him an unusual confidence in any fight, as it enabled him to win physical confrontations over opponents who far surpassed him in size. I remember a hospital visit when I first met him, when I thought his size had lost the fight, till I later found out he was fighting five guys. His strength was also the factor that drew him into the gangs, and enabled him to rise to leadership. Men feared him, rightfully so, but also from the reputation he had built. Reputation often is greater than the truth, but even at that, there was a lot of truth in the stories which had circulated about Dink. I realized now how he had risen so fast and so far in the Almandine before he was saved. I finally drifted off to sleep too.

It was about 2:00 in the morning when Dink shook me to wake me up. He immediately put his hand over my mouth and whispered, "Shhh---no noise! We're gettin outa here now!"

I figured it wouldn't do any good to ask how, in light of the need for silence and the fact I was totally dependent on him. He did give me one more instruction, as he said, "Don't take nuttin wid you now. We might be able to get it later!"

I wasn't sure what conclusions to draw from that, but my heart was already beating like a set of drums at a rock concert! No need to think any further bad thoughts now!

We made our way to the door, and to my surprise he pulled out a key and unlocked it quietly!! I wanted to ask where he had gotten the key, but this was not the time for questions. As he pushed the door open slowly, I prayed it would not make any creaking sound, and it didn't. We had no idea what was on the other side of that door! When the door was finally open, we saw that the hallway outside the door was dimly lit, but we could see the two hoods sleeping as they sat on the floor leaning against the wall---Uzis in hand (that's what Dink had called their guns)! I hoped my pounding heart would not wake them up either.

Dink crept with the greatest of stealth over to the first one, and motioned for me to do the same toward the second one. I wondered what we were going to do with them! I didn't know any karate or any kung-fu or anything. And I wasn't as strong as Dink. How was I going to put this dude out of commission? My worst nightmare now was for him to wake up in the middle of my pre-assault debate as to how I was going to assault him!

Dink motioned for me to hit him with a karate chop, and I shrugged my shoulders, raised my hand and shook my head to tell him such a move from me would only awake this sleeping giant. Dink understood, and got himself into place where he could quickly grab his assigned hood by the mouth and neck to put a twist on his head that disarmed and sent him into unconsciousness. He went so limp, I wondered if Dink had killed him! Almost in the same motion, he grabbed his Uzi before it could hit the ground---and all of this was done without any noise whatsoever.

He then came quietly to my side. He handed me the Uzi (I had no idea what to do with it---I had never fired one---I wouldn't even know how to take it off safety, if it had one), and then he applied the same procedure to my assigned hood. That left both hoods completely "discombooberated" ---a word I had learned from Dink.

I said silently within, "Praise the Lord." I wondered if it was proper to praise the Lord for "discombooberating" two guys! I was sure glad the Lord had not put me through a gangster background before He saved me!

"What now?" I mouthed to him with some relief.

"Let's see who else is here---and be careful!" he mouthed back.

We crept down the hall like two cats stalking a mouse. We passed two doors which were open, and a quick look around confirmed no one was in those rooms. We came to the "conference" room or for us the "interrogation" room, and it was open and empty also. The final question was whether there was anyone inside the huge door at the front of the bunker, which would let us out. We stopped about fifty feet from it, and Dink whispered, "There ain't nobody inside ta stop us from gettin' out now!"

"Yes, but what if there is someone outside?" I asked.

"We'll see in a second. First, Preacha, let's get our stuff," he said as he turned to walk back towards our room.

"What if those guys wake up?" I asked as we passed our "discombooberated" friends. I almost expected him to say they would never wake up on this earth again.

"No chance a dat! Deys out fer da night. And when dey do wake up, it'll be wid a lotta pain!" Dink assured me.

I must say, that statement comforted me, as killing someone was not one of my common experiences or strong points.

I began to get my stuff, but Dink warned me that we needed to travel as light as possible, because we don't know what the next few days might hold. That wasn't very encouraging! But it was too late to turn back now. I pared my stuff down as best as possible, but I did throw my Bible and notes on Job into my little bag.

Three questions remained in my mind.

Number one---how do we get past that huge front door?

Number two---where do we go when and if we do get out safely?---we don't even know where we are. Or do we?

Number three---does God's providence cover "discombooberating" people and even shooting someone with an Uzi to accomplish that noble(?) goal?---because I now had one in my hands, and I wondered if I could use it in the next few minutes if it became necessary?

I encouraged myself, as we snuck back down the hallway, by remembering David as he went against the giant---in the providence of God. Right now I felt like anyone we might meet outside would qualify as a giant---and even though I had much more than a sling-shot, I was still scared out of my wits!!!

15

Is the Dross All Cleaned Out Yet....?

I only design thy dross to consume and thy gold to refine...

Before approaching the huge front door (and I had no idea how we would try to open it), we searched each of the other rooms a second time to be sure Little Dinky was not there. We also looked for other possible rooms which would be entered in some manner not visible immediately to the human eye. We found no one and nothing---except the two sleeping hoods.

Then came my dreaded moment---we started towards the front door. I remembered when we came in that it had swung upward, and I had no idea how Dink and I could force it open. He was the expert on these matters---I was hoping and trusting.

As we approached the door, he whispered to me, "When da door opens, be ready fer any ting! Ya might have ta use dat gun ya got in yer hands! Do ya know how ta use it?"

Quickly in about thirty seconds he gave me a crash course in the use of an Uzi, concluding with the warning and a soft laugh, "Jus' don't hit me wid it!"

I assured him he was the last guy on the premises (if there were others), that I wanted to shoot. I assured him further that it would be only by God's providence that I would or could hit anything or anybody with it. I laughed as I told him to just trust God's providence.

"Preacha, dat reminds me---we'se fergetten sometin,'" he warned. "We ain't prayed yet. Lead us in prayer, Preacha, before we'se open dat door."

I felt like I needed to pray that we could even open the door, but he didn't seem to have any concern for that area of our problems. But I prayed for it any way, and for safety to everyone. My hope was that no one would be on the other side and that I would not have to use this gun in my hands. I had never killed any one before. I wasn't even a hunter. I didn't like the sight of blood, especially my own.

After I had prayed, Dink told me to get ready--- whatever he meant by that. I have never felt so unprepared for anything in all my life. Then he reached into his pocket and pulled something out. It was an automatic door opener?---like the kind one uses on a garage. I wondered to myself, "Dink, are you crazy?---using your garage door opener on this thing?" If it wasn't his garage door opener, where had he gotten it? Surely it couldn't be the garage door opener to his house? Had he stolen it from the hoods?

"Ready?" he asked.

I gave a huge sigh, not of relief, but of preparation, and nodded a "yes" as best I could.

He motioned for me to get down flat on the floor. My hand tightened on the trigger as he punched the door opener. I expected that it wouldn't open the door, but then to my surprise and horror it began to open with a huge continuous grinding noise. I wanted to turn and run back into the safety of the bunker. But I stayed, and my eyes searched and waited for someone to appear in front of the door, or to run at us as it got high enough for an entrance. But the door kept grinding until it was completely open. And then there was a dead eerie silence, which was as frightening as the roar of the door when it was opening.

"That was loud enough to raise the dead!" I whispered to Dink, with my eyes still glued to the door.

"Yeah," Dink said, "But not loud enough ta wake up dose discombooberated boys!"

"What now?" I asked eagerly. "Can we assume that no one else was here to guard us but those two hoods?"

"Yeah, its beginnin' ta look dat way," he answered. "Come on! Lets edge towards da door slowly, but you stay on dat side of da door an I'll stay on dis side."

So we began moving toward the door, one on one wall and the other pressed against the other wall. When we came to the entrance, we peered out into the darkness.

"Da helicopter pad is empty!" Dink observed.

"What does that mean?" I asked anxiously again.

"It means da two hoods probly were da only two guardin' us," he explained again.

"So what now?" I asked again, understanding why those seemed to be the only words in my vocabulary just now.

"'Well, we moves out slow-like---not straight but on da right side of da door," he said as he moved to my side of the entrance and took the lead.

When we had moved far enough in a slow manner to assure there was no one on the premises except us and the two sleeping hoods, we then began to move faster. When we reached an open field, we began to run. When we came to a wooded or thicker underbrush, we would move more slowly, but still as fast as we dared. Branches hit our faces in some places. We stumbled at times over unseen stumps and vines. We traveled in this manner about two hours, and I had no idea where we were or what direction we were going. Finally Dink motioned for us to stop, and we rested for a few moments, but neither of us could speak for a few seconds, as we were so exhausted and panting our lungs out.

Finally I had to ask, "What direction are we going?"

"South!" Dink declared without hesitation.

"What's our plan? They'll be looking for us, won't they?" I asked hoping for a "no" answer.

"Yeah! Its 'bout five o'clock, an its gonna be gettin light in an hour or so---which means we'll have ta stop and take cover!" he explained.

"Stop and take cover?" I asked with some confusion. "Don't we need to put as many miles between us and them as possible in these next hours?" I argued.

"Preacha, deys gonna come after us wid da helicopter and we'd be settin' ducks out der in da middle a one of dose fields. Besides, someone else might see us, an dat might not be too good."

"Why not?" I asked. "Maybe someone would call the police and they would come and help us!" I argued further.

"Yeah," Dink replied, "An maybe one a dose police guys might have Almandine connections!"

"What?" I returned with disbelief.

"Believe me, Preacha! I knows what I'm talkin' about!"

I didn't argue with that point. But I did ask another question.

"Dink, tell me something. Where did you get the key and the door opener to that bunker? And did you know those two goons were the only ones on the premises? Boy, what a chance we were taking, if there would have been others there."

"Preacha, I supervised da building a dat bunker!" he offered.

"You mean to say that you knew that bunker and had been there before?" I asked in amazement.

"Yep, and I made sure dat when I left da organization dat I had a secret key an a door opener, in case dey ever came after me. Dis bunker was built precisely for dat purpose---to convince deserters of da error of der ways. About da two goons, as you call dem, I figured dey was da only ones, but we had ta be sure and careful."

"If you knew that bunker, why did we search for extra rooms?" I asked.

"Cause ya never knows when dey might have added sometin' more ta da original structure," he explained.

He motioned for us to get going, so we moved out, traveling as long as we dared as the sun was rising in the east. And sure enough, I knew then we were going south. But how long and how far we would have to travel before we felt safe, I had no idea. We weren't "out of the woods" yet!---pardon the pun.

As we ran through the fields and forests, I encouraged myself by singing softly a song:

When through fiery trials thy pathway shall lie,
My grace all-sufficient shall be thy supply;
The flame shall not hurt thee; I only design
Thy dross to consume, thy gold to refine.

When we stopped to rest, Dink asked me what I had been singing. I shared the verse of the song, and he replied, "Preacha, da Lord sure has been doin' a lotta 'dross consumin' and 'gold refinin' in our lives dese past few days!"

"Yeah!" I replied with a smile. "And I feel all cleaned out of dross just now. He can stop anytime He wants. But I bow to His sovereign providence."

16

Have They Found Our Hiding Place...?

Hide me under the shadow of Thy wings....

I could tell during our last hour of travel after our five o'clock rest, that Dink had been looking for a place to hide for the day. We passed what I thought might be a good place, but we kept moving, as darkness began to fade.

I noticed also that he kept taking us through the woods, and we were traveling due east now, when we could have been traveling through the open fields and to the south. I figured he might be doing that for several reasons.

First, we were traveling through the woods to make ourselves scarce to anyone who might see us---those looking for us or those not looking for us.

Second, I figured that he might be looking for a hiding place in the woods, since there didn't seem to be any mountains or caves in this area.

Third, I assumed we were moving east, hoping any searchers might figure we had traveled due south, and this jaunt to the east might throw them off our trail a mile or so ---maybe just enough to save us.

Then suddenly he signaled for me to stop. There in front of us was one of the thickest woods I had ever seen. We entered it and traveled several hundred yards until we came upon a large fallen tree stretched out before us.

"Dat's our hiden' place, Preacha! We can crawl up under dat big tree an no one can see us from da air or from da ground even if deys right close to us."

We scrounged around under the tree to find the best and most comfortable place to hide. We crawled into our shelter not caring if it was on the ground. We could lie down in peace for some hours and rest. I was glad it was summer time, and warmer, even in the northeast, though it was cooler than an early morning at home. I was glad I had brought my jacket. It looked like it was going to be a sunny day, which seemed to be a blessing as well.

"Preacha, before we goes ta sleep, give us a lesson from Job!" Dink requested.

I gave him the material from Job 8 that I had prepared during the time they were beating him up. He seemed encouraged.

Then I asked him some questions. Dink never seemed to offer any information till you asked him.

"How far do we have to travel until we can stop running under cover? Could we get a bus or something from one of the little towns we will pass?"

"Preacha, da further we can go on our own, da less chance of dem catchin' us. Dey has lookouts in ever one of dese little towns fer miles. Da lookouts has contacts wid people who ain't even Almandine who pass on information 'bout suspicious an unexplained strangers who pass through dese little places. We may need ta travel several days before we can hop a bus. We'se gots to be safe cause if dey catch us now, its over fer both of us an Little Dinky as well."

As I thought about his statement, I tried to remember and figure out what day it was---but I couldn't. I did know that our families hadn't heard from us since the morning we left home. I longed to just go to a phone and call them and assure them we were safe, but Dink said that had its dangers also.

So I asked another question.

"Dink, when we get home, what do we do then about trying to find Little Dinky?"

"Well, I'se been tinkin an I ain't figured it all out yet. Right now, let's concentrate on gettin' to New York City and gettin' our car and goin' home!"

I couldn't disagree with that, and the sooner the better.

"Preacha, why don't ya sleep for several hours while I keep a watch for any body comin' after us. Den I can sleep while you'se watch."

It was 6:30 or so, and the morning light was invading even our hiding place, but it didn't take much to lure me to go to sleep...........!

About 10:00 I was awakened by the noise of a helicopter in the distance. Dink was still awake.

"Dink, is that the Almandine chopper we hear?" I asked immediately.

"Don't know, Preacha. We'll know in a minute as it sounds like its gettin closer!"

As we peered through the leaves of the trees, we couldn't see it, but we knew it was back west of us. It never flew directly over us, but the noise grew dimmer and then was gone.

"Deys 'bout a mile ta da west of us!" Dink explained.

"I guess our cutting east was the right move," I noted.

"Yeah, deys flyin' due south from da bunker!"

"Well, Preacha, its my turn ta sleep now, if you'se got your rest finished. You musta, cause you sure snored up a storm!" Dink said kiddingly.

When he woke up about 2:00 that afternoon, we both commented on the fact we were hungry.

"Yeah, Dink, what are we going to eat these several days?" I asked.

He smiled as he reached into his bag and pulled out some bread and roast beef and said jokingly, "Eat dis wid da blessing of da Almandine. Dey even sent some water too!" he commented as he pulled out a bottle of water.

We decided we had better ration our food for several days of travel, but even that small amount was like a steak to us.

When the meal was over, Dink asked for more from the book of Job. It was only about 4:00 by then, and we had several hours before it would be dark so we could travel, so I pulled out my notes on Job 9.

About that time we heard the helicopter again. It was coming back and sounded like it was going to pass right over us. It was stopping now about every several hundred yards scouring the ground below. and firing into the woods. Maybe they had gotten word from someone who had seen us in those early morning hours in this area.

Dink and I crawled further under the big tree. I hoped we wouldn't stir up some bed of snakes that would send us running from our hiding place. The chopper came close, and it stopped so close that the trees above us waved in the breeze of its wake. Had they seen us? Had we left a trail? Or was this just a routine procedure, as we were smack dab in the middle of this heavy thicket? What if they decided this thicket was so heavy they needed to land and comb the area on foot?

Then came the bursts of machine gun fire all over the thicket, even into the area where we were hiding!

17

Can a Man Take God to Court...?

We will not fear though the earth is cast into the sea....

As the bullets ripped through the trees, even into our big tree and into the ground around us, I kept praying for our safety and for this assault to end. It seemed like it would never stop. They must have been swinging those machine guns in every direction. The bullets would sweep all around us, then move away for a second, and then back over us. It seemed clear they were shooting in some random way, hoping to hit something.

I remembered the Biblical story about Ahab and how he died. He went into battle dressed as a common soldier and urged Jehoshaphat to lead the army. He evidently hoped that the enemy would think Jehoshaphat was Ahab, and they would not recognize Ahab as a common soldier.

But then as the army was riding by, one of the enemy drew a bow at a venture. He just saw all these enemy soldiers riding by, and drew back his bow and let it go. There wasn't much hope he would hit any body, and if he did it would be on their armor, but God guided the arrow right into the body of Ahab, through the weak place of his armor, and he died from that wound. God's providence brought Ahab to his death, though he tried to outsmart the enemy and God.

I figured that if God could guide an arrow in that manner to bring judgment on someone, He could also guide these bullets in a manner to save us. Sure enough, after they had torn up our forest thicket with their guns, they flew off, leaving Dink and me to survey any damage.

"Did dey getcha, Preacha?" he asked.

"No, how about you, Dink."

"Nah, I'se been in worse jams wid bullets flyin' when I was lost. God in His providence took care a me den, and He did again today. But if one wodda hit us, dat wodda been His providence as well. How bout dat study from Job now?"

So still shaking and surveying the damage, but confident of His providence, I began our study.

In the ninth chapter, Job answers Bildad. Remember that Bildad has told Job that he needed to get right with God because of his sin, and he has stressed that is the reason for Job's horrible condition. Bildad has been arrogant and mean in his attitude, with no compassion for Job's sufferings.

Now, how does Job answer Bildad? Does he have the same spirit of condemnation for Bildad? No, Job's answer is that he has no answers. He is only certain of one thing, and that is that he is not guilty of great sin before God as Bildad accuses him of such.

Job then asks several questions of which he does not have the answer.

1. Question One---How can a man be right with God 9:9

Job asserts that he has the works to be right with God, if salvation is by works. But, on the other hand, he says that the proof of salvation is not a life which is full of ease and free of suffering, because he has the suffering even though he has a life of godly works. Therefore, there must be another way of being right before God.

2. Question Two---Can a man argue with God   9:3-10

There are two problems in arguing with God, according
to Job. First, if a man argues with God, God will not
answer him except once in a thousand times. Second,
God is much greater and stronger than man. A man had
better consider who God is before he tries to argue with
Him.

> He is stronger than man   4
>> Who has hardened himself before God
>>> and prospered?
> He removes mountains   5
> He shakes the earth out of its place   6
> He commands the sun and it rises not   7
> He seals up the stars   7
> He alone spreads out the heavens   8
> He treads upon the waves of the sea   8
> He makes the spaces of the heavens   9
> He does great things past finding out   10
> He performs wonders without number   10
> Who can argue with a God like this?

3. Question Three---Can a man stand up to God? 9:11-13

This seems similar to arguing with God, but it may carry
more of a legal connotation. Can a man take God into
court to charge Him, to challenge Him, to bring Him
into account for His actions? What if God does something I do not like. Can a man take Him to court? A
man might threaten to, but he is wasting his time even

thinking or talking about it, and he is beyond doubt amassing God's judgment unto himself. No man can call God to court because:

> He goes by and I see Him not   11
> He takes away possessions, life, etc.   12
>> who can hinder Him?
>> who can say, "What are You doing?"
> He does not restrain His anger   13
>> even the proud helpers bow at His feet

4. Question Four---Can a man answer God?   9:14-17

When God speaks or has spoken, can a man answer Him?

> How much less shall I answer Him?   14
> How can I choose words to reason with Him?   14
> Though I were righteous   15
>> I would not argue with Him
>> I would make supplication to Him as my judge
> If I had called and He had answered me   16-17
>> I would not believe He has answered my voice
>>> because He breaks me with a tempest
>>> because he multiplies my wounds
>>>> without a cause

5. Question Five---Does a man have any course to God in his suffering except to become bitter?   9:18-20

The answer which comes at this point may be no higher than human reason can reach---the answer of one who does not exercise faith in God's person and ways.

> Have I any course but bitterness   18-20
>> He will not let me get my breath   18
>>> but He overwhelms me with misery
>>> (maybe bitterness here)
>> He is stronger than I am   19
>> He refuses to consider my case   19
>> He knows I do not claim perfection   20

Job is right in this conclusion. For if a man lives without faith, such a man will come to no other conclusions than those above.

6. Question 6---Can a man claim a knowledge of God's ways? 9:21-24

(in the following section, the words in parentheses are additions from implication of the context)

I am innocent   21
>   (yet I suffer---who can explain it?)

I know not my soul   21
>   (I am puzzled!)

I despise my life   21
>   (what good is it or what purpose does it fulfill?)

Therefore I must conclude
>   God destroys both the upright and the wicked
>   God will laugh at the despair of the innocent   23
>>   if the scourge kills one suddenly
>   God blindfolds the judges   24
>>   when the earth is given over to the wicked

(Again the above is the highest human reason can reach)

7. Question Seven---Can a man argue sensibly before men
   while in such ignorance?   9:25-31

   Job acknowledges that he is speaking in ignorance
      (the ignorance of human reason)

   my ignorance is apparent   25-31
      my days are swifter than a runner   25-26
         they flee away
         they see no good or joy
         they slip past like swift boats   26
         they speed like an eagle hastening to prey   26
      I can't change my mind about my sorrow   27-28
         I cannot forget my complaints   27
         I cannot leave off my heaviness   27
         I cannot comfort myself   27
         I am still in my sorrows and dread them   28
         I still know you will condemn me   28
      if I cleanse my hand with snow   30-31
         you (his friends?) plunge me into the mud pit
            so that my own clothes hate me

Summary
   a man cannot argue with God
   a man cannot take God to court
   a man cannot answer God
   a man can only come to bitterness
      against God and His ways
   a man can have no knowledge
      of God and His ways
   a man not only cannot argue with God
      but he cannot argue with men either
      while in such a state of ignorance

Final thoughts   9:32-35

> God is not a man as I am   32
>> that I could answer Him
>> that we could take Him to court
> Neither is there any mediator between us   33-34
>> to lay his hand on us both to bring us together
>> to take God's rod away from me
>> to remove His terror from me
> Then would I speak up and not fear Him   35
>> but that is not the case at the present
> Thus any attempts
>> to understand God's ways are hopeless
>> to justify man's ways are hopeless
> Thus man must wait upon God
>> for any answer
>> for any hope

When I had finished, Dink remarked, "Whew, Preacha, dat sure is us, ain't it? We can't understand God's ways! We cannot justify our ways---we'se too sinful. Human reason comes ta da wrong answers. Da answers must come from God. Well, let's get some sleep fer an hour or so and den take off an see how far we can get tonight!"

I had to admit that the thought of starting off again in the dark through unknown fields and thickets did not sound inviting in any way. The night before I had existed on adrenaline. But tonight I was tired and weary. But then Jesus must have been weary too. A verse came to my mind:

> *Consider Him who endured such contradiction*
> *of sinners against Himself....*
> *Hebrews 12:3*

18

Can Truth and Error Bless Us...?

We were pressed out of measure....

When the full darkness arrived, we took off on our night journey. My legs and whole body were sore from the previous evening of flight, but the necessity of the hour seemed to carry me along through the dark fields and forests. We did head south, moving quickly, but not on the run as we had been last night. We steered clear of the main roads, houses and cities and villages, sometimes having to detour a bit from our southward course.

After several hours we stopped to rest, and I asked Dink some more questions.

"How far south do we have to go before we can feel safe and take to the main roads? What if we come to a river that we need to cross?"

"Well, somewhere out der in fronta us der should be an interstate highway," he explained. "When we gets ta dat, we'll find us a motel an get cleaned up an sleep in a bed, an den we'll take a bus ta de city!"

"But what do we do for money?" I asked again. "The Almandine took our wallets!"

He reached into his bag and pulled out something, threw it to me, and, lo and behold, it was my wallet.

"How did you get this?" I asked incredulously.

"Same way I got da food an some other stuff. I jus' took it! I tink dey owed us dat much."

We took off again, but before we did I asked, "How far did you say that interstate was?"

"I didn't say!" he responded. "Maybe we can hit it tomorrow night sometime. It all depends on what we'se run inta out here."

As the night wore on, my legs got heavier by the mile. And they began to cramp and ache. The rest stops helped, but each time after some rest, it was more difficult to get going again. I don't think I have ever spent a longer or more miserable night. But, praise the Lord, it was an uneventful though painful stroll in the dark. I couldn't wait for the sun to begin to appear, which would force us to stop!

Finally we headed for the thickest forest or clump of trees we could find, entered it, and found a hiding place. There always seems to be an old tree under which one could hide. Dink seemed tired also (I could tell it in his speech). As we stretched out to talk and watch the dawning of the new day, I began rubbing my legs, and I really wondered if I could revive them enough to go the next evening. I thought maybe conversation would help me forget the pain.

"Do you think they have quit looking for us?" I asked hopefully.

"Well, dey may not be lookin' fer us, but some body is!" he said with conviction.

"By 'dey' you mean the thugs, I take it, but who is the some body?" I asked again.

"Da Almandine got more helpers dan you'd imagine. See da lights of dat house over der in da distance? Dose folks could be contact people fer da Almandine. An I guarantees you dat dey gots da word out ta all der contacts ta be on da lookout fer two guys walkin' south."

"Do the contact people ever come into the woods and fields looking for escapees from the Almandine like us?" I asked with some concern.

"Oh, yeah, Preacha! Dey kinda makes a huntin game outa it!" he explained further.

"A hunting game!!!" I repeated.

"Yeah, you know, kinda like huntin' deer, or some other kinda animal. Dey use dogs an da whole bit---a real sport fer dem!"

"Dogs!!!" I said with a wince. I had to admit that I was not a dog lover. In fact I was close to a dog-hater, since I had been bitten by one on a lonely country road a few years ago. He wasn't a big one either. I didn't know what I would do if a big one came at me!!

"Dink, this sounds like a regular routine for the Almandine---for them to have lookout houses to help them detain their enemies."

"Sure!" he offered, "And it works both ways!"

"Both ways? What do you mean?" I queried again.

"Well, da lookout folks watch fer people comin' out and goin' in---especially when dey has been informed of a potential problem!" he explained again.

"Dink, one more question! Has anyone ever got past the lookout people going in or out?" I asked, not sure if I really wanted the answer.

"Nope! Not ta my knowledge. Not when I was workin' wid da Almandine."

I had been feeling safer since we had moved further from the bunker, but that feeling disappeared, and I wasn't sure if I could sleep through the day or not. What if one of these "huntin" parties crept up on us---and with dogs!

Then Dink suggested we look at Job so we could keep up our spiritual strength. And so I opened my notes and began.

The theme of chapter ten of Job is that true thoughts and false thoughts cannot bring comfort to a suffering man. The false thoughts will derail the true thoughts all the time, and rob them of their power to encourage him.

"Boy, den let's pray we can have true thoughts taday--- we sure needs encouragement!" Dink urged.

Then I listed Job's true and false thoughts.

I   A CLEAR REALITY---JOB HATES HIS
     CONDITION   10:1

     My soul hates my life
          therefore I will give free reign
               to my complaints
          therefore I will speak
               from the bitterness of my soul
     Observation
          this is rather typical of man

II   A CLEAR FAILURE---JOB DEPENDS ON
     HUMAN REASON AND THE RESULT IS
     A COMBINATION OF TRUTH AND ERROR
     BUT NO COMFORT   10:2-18

     A. False Thought   2

          Job asks God not to condemn him
               but God is not condemning him
               God is only testing him

B. False Thought 2

Job asks God to show him the charges
    and the reason God fights against him
but again God has not brought any charges
    God is not fighting against him
    God has only spoken the highest of him
thus silence from God does not mean
    that He has or is condemning us

C. False Thought 3

Job asks if it is good for God to oppress him
    while God blesses the schemes of the wicked
but again God is not oppressing him
    God is for him
    God is shaping him
    God is not despising the work of his hands
    God praises his godliness
    God just doesn't always and immediately
        show his reward by human means
    God wants us to obey and walk by faith

D. False Thought 4-6

God, are You looking at me
    without omniscience?
        through the eyes of a man
        from the limited view of man

E. True Thought 7

Job quickly corrects himself
>God, you are omniscient
Therefore
>You know that I am not guilty
>You know that no one can deliver me
>>out of your hand

F. True Thoughts and False Thoughts Mixed in
    an Abundance   9-12

True
>You are my Creator   8
False
>Will You now come and destroy me?
>Why did You create me
>>if You intended to kill me

True
>You made me from clay   9
False
>Will you now turn me into dust?   9
>>in the grave?
>Have you poured me out like milk?   10
>>Am I of no further use to You
>>>that you would just discard me?
>Have you curdled me like cheese?   10
>>Am I sour and rotten to You now?

True
>You have clothed   11
>>me with skin and flesh
>You have knit me together   11
>>with bones and sinews

You have given me life and favor   12
You have preserved my spirit with care   12

G. A Question Which Must Be Faced and
    Answered   13-15

Question   13
    If You are my Creator
        why are You doing these things to me?
Answers   13
    You have hidden the reasons
        in your heart
Possibilities
    If I have sinned   14
        then you have marked me for judgment
        then you will not acquit me of my sins
    If I have been wicked   15
        woe unto me   15
    If I am innocent   15
        I still cannot lift up my head
        I am full of confusion
            as to why You do this to me
        I am drowning in my affliction

H. False Thoughts   16-17

You never let me up   16
    from sending affliction upon me
You hunt me like a fierce lion   16
You display Your awesome power   16
    against me
You send new witnesses against me   17
You increase Your wrath upon me   17

You send Your forces of war   17
   to battle against me

I.   True Thought and False Thought   18-19

True
   You are my Creator   18
False
   I should have died at birth   18
   I should have been as one not born   19

I commented to Dink, "No wonder Job was so confused and so questioning of God. He allowed His thinking to be mixed with truth and error. Only truth can give a believer the victory. Error mixed with truth will always torpedo the truth and establish the error. Truth will never gain the victory if mixed with error."

"Thanks, Preacha! Da truth is dat God is in control an workin' His providence in all tings---even in da most negative an heart-breakin' mysterious experiences a life--- even in da kidnappin' of Little Dinky!" Dink declared as he began to cry and yet praise God at the same time.

"Yes, and He's in control and working His will as the Almandine chase us!" I declared boldly. I then repeated my favorite line of poetry:

My Father's way may twist and turn,
My heart may throb and ache!
But in my soul, I'm glad I know,
God maketh no mistake.

With that we rejoiced and settled down to rest. But then our ears picked up a very unwelcome sound!

19

Can a Barking Dog Bring Any Good...?

Jesus led me all the way....

The unwelcome sound was that of a dog barking in the distance. My first thought was that they are coming with the dogs for us. But then I realized it could be a dog just barking from afar in his back yard, or as he roamed the territory. Just so he stayed away from us!

I noticed that Dink had straightened up also, and was listening.

"What is that?" I asked with definite concern.

"Its a dog!" he answered smiling at me.

"Yes, I know its a dog, Dink. But is it a dog looking for us?" I said clarifying my question.

"Yeah, I tink so!" he spoke ruining my rest and morning.

"What do we do?" I asked again, trying to rest in God's providence. I noted in my mind that it is very easy to trust in the providence of God when all is going well, but when the test comes, the natural mind wants some answers. I was glad we had just gone over the Word of God, and that certainly made it easier to turn it over to Him, even though my heart was still racing.

Dink answered me interrupting my thinking.

"We'll jus' wait an see. Maybe its nuttin. Maybe we can get da jump on whoever it is. Or maybe...."

He didn't finish that sentence as a man came into view in the distant field, and he was coming straight at us---with a dog!! And as he got closer I could see there was a gun in his hand---a shotgun!!

"What do we do!!" I asked Dink again.

"Jus' sit tight an see who he is an what he does!" Dink advised.

The woods we were in weren't really that big, or we could have moved further into them. We were about fifty feet into the brush, and had a fairly clear view of the approaching man---and his dog!

Then the dog began to bark, as if he had picked up our scent. I was glad he was on a leash, but by now he was really straining to run towards us and get at us. Then Dink, so my surprise, called to the man.

"Jimmy! Is dat you?"

"Yeah! Who is that in there?" he returned.

"Its Dink!"

"Hey, man, I didn't know we were looking for you!" Jimmy responded. "Come on out of there. I've got the dog."

I looked at Dink and asked, "Can we trust him? Is he an Almandine lookout or a friend?"

"Oh yeah, we can trust him. He's both!"

I didn't quite know what to make of that last statement, but nonetheless we crawled out of the woods carrying our few possessions, and Dink and Jimmy hugged one another, and exchanged a few comments concerning old times.

"Man, am I glad ta see you!" Dink said.

"Ditto, Dink old boy! I'll never forget what you did for me years ago! You're a friend for life. Who's this fellow with you?" he asked.

"Jimmy, dis is my preacha, Ira Pointer. Preacha, dis is Jimmy Masters---a true friend if der ever was one."

"Your preacher?" Jimmy echoed. "I heard you had gotten religion. I wouldn't believe it until now. It had to come from your own lips. Is that what we're after you for? For getting religion?"

And believe it or not, then and there Dink witnessed to him explaining that he hadn't gotten religion, but Jesus Christ the risen Lord had gotten hold of him. He pressed Jimmy for a decision after we had spent about twenty minutes talking about Jimmy's need of salvation. I must confess, I was getting a little uneasy, though they acted like it was old homecoming day at church. What if the copter flew by? Or what if Dink made Jimmy mad? We were pretty well in Jimmy's hands. But then nothing was as important to Dink as the souls of men. At times he put me to shame.

Jimmy was a big man, about six feet four inches tall, and he weighed about two hundred and sixty pounds. He was about fifty years old or so. He was outward in his personality and jovial in his demeanor, and evidently Dink had befriended him at some earlier point in their lives when Dink was in the Almandine. God's providence again was made evident to us.

Dink told Jimmy how the Almandine had kidnapped his son, and how we had come to talk to Frankie to try to get him back. They had taken us to the bunker, but we had escaped, and had been running for two nights.

Jimmy shook his head and exclaimed, "Boy, you guys sure made the time those two nights. It has taken most guys I catch three days to get this far---if they make it. Come on! You guys must be hungry and tired."

I was a little skeptical about walking through an open field, and so was Dink. So Jimmy walked off into the distance with the promise that he would get his truck and come back for us. We took refuge in our brush again.

I couldn't help but wonder about Jimmy coming back for us as promised.

"Dink, what if Jimmy brings some Almandine men back with him?" I asked suspiciously.

"Jimmy? Never!! Dat's a big ου μη in da Greek!"

That was an expression we both knew from the study of Greek together. It expresses a double negative in the Greek, which is an emphatic negative. I always jokingly translated it as "never ever, under any circumstances, at any time, at any place, anywhere." So Dink was saying to me that Jimmy would never ever, under any circumstance, at any time, any place, any where betray us and bring the Almandine back.

I must admit that did comfort me, and sure enough it wasn't long until Jimmy was back, and we were in his truck, traveling to his home for food and rest. We did have to ride in the bed covered with a canvas, in case we came in contact with other Almandine members or lookouts.

I thought to myself, how's that for the providence of God! I asked Dink what it was he had done for Jimmy that made him such a friend---even to risk his own neck for us.

He said that one day when he came to the bunker on Almandine business, three of the underling hoods were beating up on Jimmy, and even had a gun to his head, and would probably have killed him.

"Why, what had he done?" I asked.

"One of da hoods had attacked his daughter, an Jimmy had come to da bunker ta call him on it. So instead of da hood facin' Jimmy alone, which was da Almandine rules, all three of da hoods jumped him. When I got der I demanded to know what was goin' on. Jimmy told me, and I commanded dem to stop an jus' let Jimmy an da guilty hood duke it out. Well, dat didn't satisfy dem, so dey all took on Jimmy and me. We cleaned der plows an Jimmy became a friend fer life. He figures he owes me his life."

I thought again of the providence of God. The event just described by Dink. The pathway of our travel for two nights from the bunker. The presence of Jimmy that very day looking for us not knowing who we were. His finding us when others were no doubt looking also. Our being in that very place at that very time and Jimmy being there also. That is the providence of God!

When we got to Jimmy's house, we met his wife, and she was more excited to see Dink than Jimmy had been, if that was possible. She couldn't do enough for us---she served the biggest breakfast I have ever had in my life. The biggest smiles and friendliness ever seen. And the continual assurance that we were safe and they would get us to New York. And, finally, a hot bath and then two beds in the upstairs of that big farmhouse with the softest mattress and pillows one could ever imagine.

It didn't take me long to go to sleep, thinking little of the ache in my legs or the travel ahead of us. I did long to call Terry, but that would have to wait until we were further out of the Almandine territory. I could only praise His glorious grace and providence that had spared us.

Through all eternity to Thee,
A joyful song I'll raise;
But, oh, eternity's too short,
To utter all Thy praise.
Joseph Addison

20

Can God Save a Wretch Like Me...?

I've wandered far away from God....

We slept till about 4:00 in the afternoon---the best sleep I had experienced in days. Jimmy was going to try to smuggle us out after it got dark. So we got up, cleaned up again, and went down to supper. Dink asked me to bring our Bible study material on Job.

Janice, Jimmy's wife, had prepared another fantastic meal. To be honest, I didn't know if I could eat much. We had been rationing our food the last several days, even doing without at times, and my stomach had shrunk. It still felt full from breakfast. But we did enjoy the meal, and I ate more than I thought I could---fried chicken and all the trimmings.

Then Dink said, "Preacha, get out yer Bible an notes an let's study da Word wid Jimmy and Janice!" Nothing like Dink's boldness.

They gave no objection, and I opened my Bible and notes, wondering what the next subject matter was in chapter eleven, and how I could apply it to lost people. Looking at my notes, I was amazed once again at the providence of God. It was a study that I could apply to the hearts of the saved and the lost.

The theme was amazing---the difficulty of challenging and changing the minds of men who are in falsehood!

I gave some background on the book of Job for our hosts' sake, and then plunged into the study.

I told them that Zophar is the third friend of Job to speak to him about his great suffering being caused by his great sin. But these men would not listen to the truth---their minds were already made up. They were absolutely wrong in their thinking, but they were absolutely convinced that they were right.

Then I asked the question:

Why is it
    that falsehood is more easily believed than the truth?
    that the ones holding falsehood are more militant
        to promote it than the ones who hold the truth?
    that more men have probably died for falsehood
        than have ever died for believing the truth?

I then called their attention to how convinced Zophar was that he was right:

he is convinced that Job is lying   11:2
he is convinced that he must answer Job   11:3
he is convinced that Job is not pure   11:4
he is convinced Job must be answered by God   11:5-6
    if he will not hear men
he says Job is too philosophical   11:7-12
    can Job find out all about God by searching?   7
    can Job find out the Almighty to perfection?   8-10
        the wisdom of God is higher than the heavens   8
            (what can Job do to understand God?)
        the wisdom of God is deeper than hell   8
            (what can Job know?)

> the wisdom of God cannot be measured   9
>> it is longer than the earth
>> it is broader than the sea
> the wisdom of God cannot be questioned   10
>> if He cuts off a man---no questions
>> if He shuts a man up---no questions
>> if He gathers men together---no questions
>> who can hinder Him?

Note---this is exactly what Job has said, but his friends have not understood him. They wait for him to finish so they can accuse him again, not even courteous enough to hear him. That is how certain they are of their thinking.

> can Job fool God? 11-12
>> God knows vain men (like Job)
>> God sees wickedness also (like Job's)
>> God takes note of all of this---vanity and sin
>> God knows vain men would try to be wise
>>> though man has no basis of wisdom
>>> by his birth

But not only is Zophar convinced that Job must be answered because he is lying, but he is also convinced that Job must repent, and then all will be well (11:13-19)

> Job must get right with God   13-14
> Job can then approach God   15
> Job will then be rid of his misery   16-19

Thus the message of Zophar is the same as his friends:
> Job must be guilty---he is suffering greatly
> Job is wrong in his theology---see what it gets him

Job must get right with God---then suffering will go
Job will be judged if he does not repent

Thus the message of Zophar also would say
    I am not guilty of sin---I am healthy
    I am right in my theology---see what I have
    I must be right with God---all is well
    I don't need to repent---I have ease and comfort

The truth was:
    Job is a sinner but not the depraved reprobate that
        his friends see him to be
    Job is suffering but not because of the sin
        his friends think he has
    his friends are the guilty sinners
        because they condemn Job
        because their theology is wrong
        because they need repentance
        because they are blind to the truth

I closed our study by driving it home, asking us all to note the following:

Men who are separated from God
    always think they are right with God
        or they don't need God
    always think they know more than God
        and more than His word
    always refuse to come to God by faith
        because they think their beliefs are sufficient
    always hold their falsehood with strong conviction
        even though it will drag them into hell
        and even though they argue its truth till death

> always are offended when someone tries
>> to present them the truth
>> and lead them to the Word of God
>> and introduce them to the Son of God
> always think they are better
>> than those who know God
>> than those who know the truth of God
> always persecute and even assault
>> those who are right with God
>> those who are seeking to help them
>>> get right with God

I looked over at Janice and Jimmy, and they had tears in their eyes. As we talked they spoke of becoming bitter against God and rejecting Him---all of this because of the disappearance of their daughter at the hands of the Almandine.

They explained that after Jimmy and Dink had beat up on the three hoods, the Almandine came and took their daughter away (she was only nineteen years old). It was all about the time Dink had left the organization, when he became a Christian, and they didn't know where to reach him for help. The Almandine had kept them in line for years with the assurance that their daughter was all right, but they as parents had no idea if that was true or where she was. Jimmy said with tears that this is the reason he was so glad to see Dink again. Maybe Dink could help them find their daughter.

Dink assured them he was going to turn the world upside down, if possible, to find Little Dinky, and he would also search for their daughter. But then he challenged them that there was a greater matter before them---what would they do with God's Son, the Lord Jesus Christ. They had been bitter against God for years, but now was the time to come to Christ in repentance and faith and receive the forgiveness of their sins. God does not promise that He will send their daughter back to them, but God is God, and He will do what is right. Their obligation is to let God be God, and bow to Him---His power and authority, and the authority of His Word, and the authority of His Son.

Jimmy by now was bawling his eyes out, and said to us, "Can God save an old wretch like me?"

Dink explained their situation and need further, assuring them of God's grace to the vilest sinner, and then we all got on our knees together. It was like God had been preparing their hearts for years! We cried out to Him and something took place in their hearts that night as they bowed to the Lord Jesus Christ as the Spirit of God wrought a work of regeneration, giving them the gifts of repentance and faith.

No doubt about it---they were changed when we got up!!! Old Jimmy had a new smile, and Janice couldn't praise God enough. And Dink and I came to a deeper understanding of the providence of God. All of this agony and sorrow we had gone through and were going through, was God's way to get us in contact with Jimmy and Janice so we could point them to Christ and salvation.

The wanderer no more will roam,
The lost one to the fold has come,
The prodigal is welcomed home;
O Lamb of God, in Thee!

21

Who's That Kid Next to You...?

And the Lord shall guide thee continually....

After further rejoicing, we gathered our things and headed toward Jimmy's garage. It was quite dark now. We got into the back seat and crouched down and even had some empty sacks we could pull over us---just in case.

We had decided that Jimmy would take us to the interstate, which was about an hour's drive, and that he would leave us at a motel. He wanted to take us all the way to New York, but that was about a three hour drive. We didn't think it was wise for him to be gone six hours. Two hours, maybe, but not six. We would then catch a bus the next day to New York---the Lord willing.

As we drove I had to praise God's providence once again. If it had not been for His leading us to Jimmy, I would have had to walk all those miles we were going to consume in about an hour---through fields and woods and over some hills---to say nothing about His providence in saving Jimmy and Janice. God's timing and direction IS perfect.

Jimmy chatted with us from the front seat, even asking if it might be a possibility for him to move to our city and be a member of our church. He didn't know of any Christians in his area, and if he did, they probably wouldn't trust him, in light of his association with the Almandine. Also he needed to get out of his area because of that group, and maybe he thought he could help us find Dink's son and his daughter. We told him by all means to come and join us.

All was going well until we hit the first town, in fact the only town of any size between us and the interstate.

"We may be in trouble now, boys!" Jimmy exclaimed. "There's a road block ahead and some body's checking the cars."

"Can ya tell who it is?" Dink asked.

"No, and its too late to get out of this line of traffic!" Jimmy informed us.

"Could we sneak outa da car an into da field an meet ya on da other side a town?" Dink asked.

"No, too late for that too. Someone would see you and turn us in," Jimmy explained.

"Well, only one ting ta do den! We'se gotta go through it!" Dink decided.

"What's yer guess who it is?" Dink asked Jimmy?

"Its the police all right," he stated. "The only question is, what are they doing? Are they acting for the Almandine or for some other reason?"

"Would they act for the Almandine?" I asked totally uninformed about the whole situation.

"You can go ta da bank wid dat!" Dink replied.

"Preacha!" he went on. "You crawl inta da front seat an put on dis old farmer jacket, an I'll hide in under da sacks back here. If dey is lookin' fer us, dey's lookin fer two. Plus, dey wouldn't be as likely ta know you as dey would me. And further, dey ain't looking fer no farmer boy. Preacha, look as much like a farmer boy as ya can."

I wondered to myself, how do you look like a farmer boy? I did put on the coat and Jimmy gave me his hat, and I told Dink that now at least I felt like a "farmer boy." We all laughed, which helped break the tension.

Slowly our car crept towards the road block. They were only stopping the cars going our way. My first thought was that this was bad luck, but then I reminded myself that with God there is no such thing as luck. Luck speaks of chance, and with God there are no chance happenings. This was His providence, and all His providence is good.

Jimmy rolled down the window as the officer approached our car.

"Hey, Billy, what's going on out here tonight?" he asked.

"Well it seems like some boys escaped from prison up north aways, and there is an all points bulletin out for their arrest. Just routine stuff. Who's that kid next to you, Jimmy?" he asked.

"Oh, just a relative from down south. I'm taking him to the interstate to catch the bus," Jimmy explained leisurely. I thought to myself, "Well I am now his brother in Christ, and I am from down south!"

"Hey, by the way, you haven't seen Dink lately, have you? I know you and he were good friends until he disappeared when he got religion."

"Oh, I sure would love to see Dink!" Jimmy replied.

"Well, the word is out, and I guess you got it, that he and some other fellow escaped from the bunker the other night."

Then Billy leaned over closer to the car and said almost in a whisper, "Just in case you might happen to run into Dink, tell him I have some information which he needs to know."

"Well, why don't you tell me, just in case I might happen to see him!" Jimmy suggested casually.

"Well, I guess it would be all right!" he said, seeming reluctant to divulge the information. "Tell him that Frankie is dead and Geraldo is now the head man of the Almandine! Plus, tell him to contact me for information as to where they have taken his kid."

With that he waived us on, and though I am sure Dink would like to have talked to him about that last matter, we moved on through the town and out the other side, quite happy for the darkness which surrounded the winding country road.

I turned to Dink with a question.

"Well, did that last conversation with Billy tell you any thing, and does it change our plans?"

"Nah, ya can't trust old Billy. He's a born liar---a scheming, crafty, manipulative, con man. He was jus' tryin' ta feather his own cap in case Jimmy were ta see me. Am I right on dat one, Jimmy?" he asked.

Jimmy agreed.

I leaned back and began to think of some way to call home when we got to the motel. I also thought about the suffering Dink had been through. It was amazing that he had faced this trial is such a victorious manner. I tried to analyze what it was that had given him the victory. I had seen so many people go to pieces in trials. They would brood in despair, question God because of their desperation, threaten to quit in the midst of the hopelessness, at least the seeming hopelessness which they had concluded by the probing and analysis of human reason. But not Dink.

He had accepted the event as part of God's plan and providence for his life. The mystery still remained, however, for even submitting to God's trial and providence does not always remove the mystery of it all. But he had not just accepted the event in some stoic, teeth-gnashing manner. Rather he had sanctified it as from the Lord, and was seeking to resolve the problem, best he could, and he was leaving the results in the hands of the Lord. I had seen in him the triumph of faith over feelings, hope over helplessness, prayer over self-pity, and the Word of God over the threat of men before him.

Sooner than I realized it, I saw the lights of the interstate ahead, and motels and fast-food places all around us. We had made it! Dink guided Jimmy to a motel and we pulled into the parking lot. It looked like an average kind of place---not the best and not the worst---with a familiar name of a chain like those we had down our way.

I put my own coat back on, and went in to register.

Soon we were saying good bye to Jimmy, which was a time of tears. Then we went to our room and stretched out on the bed. It was a room that you entered from the outside, which might give us an opportunity to keep an eye on traffic coming and going in the parking lot. Dink was still a little skittish, or maybe cautious would be a better word.

Dink spoke up as we were so full of rejoicing.

"Preacha, give us another of dose poems or songs ya quote all da time."

The man who walks with God
always gets to his destination.

"Is dat a big "h" on his, or a little one?" Dink asked.
"Well, either way its true!" I replied rejoicingly.

The man who walks with God
always gets to His destination.

22

Is Man Really That Weak...?

I will not fear what man can do unto me....

After resting a few minutes, and not being able to sleep any way, Dink suggested we study the Word. No doubt about his regeneration---few loved the Word and witnessing like he did. Then I made my request.

"Dink, do you think there might be some way we could call home in a safe manner?"

"Yeah, we can't call our own houses, cause the Almandine might have da phones tapped. But we could call some body else---they can't tap ever body. Whodda ya suggest?" he asked.

"Well, I was thinking we might call Bob Motley, the chairman of our elder board," I suggested.

"Do it dis way!" he suggested. "Call and quickly give Bob da message. Tell him we'll be home in two ta three days, if all goes well. Tell him ta assure our wives we'se all right, but we caint call dem now. Tell him an dem to not tell any body any ting. We'll explain it all when we gets home."

And that's what I did, but it was hard to get Bob off the phone. I almost had to hang up in his face. Understandably, everyone was deeply concerned about us.

Then we turned to the study of the Word.

I began by reminding Dink that in our last study in chapter eleven that we had seen how quickly and firmly men

hold to falsehood as evidenced in Zophar's speech to Job.
Now in chapters twelve and thirteen Job answers Zophar.

The theme of this next section is that the minds of men
who hold falsehood must be challenged by the truth.

I noted first something of Job's attitude in this section:

I JOB'S ATTITUDE TOWARD ZOPHAR

A. Job is sarcastic   12:2

he tells Zophar no doubt he has all the truth
  and the truth will die with him

B. Job is confident in his knowledge as well   12:3

he says he has understanding as well as Zophar
he is not inferior to him in wisdom

II JOB'S KNOWLEDGE SHARED WITH ZOPHAR
12:4-24

A. Job lists some of the truths that he knows

he knows that his neighbors mock him   12:4
he knows that he is upright before God   12:4
he knows   12:5
    that in the thought of the one who is blessed
    there is contempt for the one suffering
he knows that those who rob others' tents   12:6
    are often prosperous
he knows that those are secure   12:7
    who provoke God by their sins

he knows that God is behind his sorrows 12:7-9
    ask the beasts of the field   7
    ask the fowls of the air   7
    speak to the earth   8
    ask the fish of the sea   8
    every one knows the truth except men
he knows that God is sovereign over all 12:9-24
    He rules over all of life   10
        every living thing is in His hand
    He rules with an ultimate wisdom   12-13
    He rules with His sovereign power 14-25
        He breaks something down   14
            and it cannot be built again
        He imprisons a man   14
            and there can be no escape
        He withholds waters   15
            and they dry up
        He looses the waters   15
            and they overrun the earth
        He has strength and wisdom   16
        He possesses the deceived and deceiver 16
        He leads counselors away empty   17
        He makes judges into fools   17
        He removes shackles put on by kings   18
        He ties the kings around the waist   18
        He leads princes away stripped   19
        He overthrows the mighty men   19
        He silences the mouths of counselors 20
        He removes the discernment of elders 20
        He floods princes with contempt   21
        He weakens the powerful   21
        He reveals the deep things of darkness   22
        He turns the deep shadows into light   22

He increases and blesses nations   23
He destroys the nations also   23
He builds nations and then destroys them   24
He takes away the wisdom of leaders   24
He sends leaders into uncertainty   24
He makes leaders stumble in darkness   24
He makes them stumble like drunkards   24

III JOB'S CHALLENGE TO ZOPHAR   13:1-19

Job challenges Zophar to understand
that they both know that God is sovereign   1-2
that he desires to speak to God   3
that his friends are liars   4-5
that they need to listen to him   6-19
do not try to speak for God   7-10
fear God instead   11-12
hold your peace that Job may speak   13:13
let Job trust in God and God alone   13:14-15
Though He slay me, yet will I trust Him
understand that God is Job's salvation   16-19

IV JOB CRIES OUT TO GOD FOR HELP   13:20-28 and 14:1-15

A. A plea to God for several things   13:20-23

Do not withdraw your hand far from me   13:20
Stop frightening me with the dread of Thee   13:21
Speak to me and let me answer Thee   13:22
Show me my transgression and sin   13:23

B. A plea to God in the form of questions   13:24-25

Why do You hide your face from me?   13:24
Why do You treat me like an enemy?   13:24
Would You torment a wind-blown leaf?   13:25
Would You pursue the dry chaff?   13:25

C. A plea to God in the form of accusations   13:26-27

You write bitter things against me   13:26
You make me guilty of the sins   13:26
    of my youth
You put my feet in shackles   13:27
You watch all my paths   13:27
You put marks on the heels of my feet   13:27

D. A plea to God in light of the above results   13:28

Job wastes away like something rotten and useless
Job wastes away like a piece of cloth eaten by moths

E. A plea to God in light of man's frailty   14:1-15

man is not the strong creature he thinks he is 14:1-2
    he is born of woman
    he lives a few days which are full of trouble
    he comes forth like a flower
        he is cut down
        he flees like a shadow
        he is gone

man sadly attempts to play God   14:3-4
    will you fix your eye on such a weak person? 3
        Job to Zophar

will you bring him before you to judge?   3
    Job to Zophar
can a clean thing come from an unclean thing 4
    Job to Zophar
        concerning Zophar's attempts upon Job

man is really controlled by God   14:5
    man's days are determined by God
    man's number of months are in God's hands
    man's boundaries are appointed by God
        man cannot pass them

man must not rebuke man in his sad estate   14:6
    look away from man in his sad estate
        a reference to Job
            Don't bug me!
                if you can't encourage me
    let me rest
        till his day is accomplished
        like a hired servant

man without the truth is like a tree   14:7-12
    the tree   7-9
        if it is cut down
            it will sprout again
            its tender branch will not cease
        though its roots grow old in the ground
            and it dies
        it will bud at the scent of water   9
        it will bring forth boughs like a plant   9
    a man   10-12
        man dies and wastes away   10
        man expires and where is he?   10

      man is like the waters   11
         which fall from the sea
      man is like the flood   11
         which decays and dries up
      man lies down and rises not   12
      man shall not awake or be raised 12
         out of sleep
         till the heavens be no more

Conclusion

The result of man's sad condition is that he is dependent upon God for all things

a. for death   13

    Oh, that You would hide me in the grave
    Oh, that you would appoint me a set time
        and then remember me

b. for protection from God's wrath   13

    Oh, that you would conceal me
        till your wrath is past

c. for resurrection   14-15

    If a man dies, shall he live again?
    I will wait all the days of my appointed time
        till my change comes
    You will call and I will answer You
    You will have a desire for the creature
        the one you made with your hands

> Thus man is a weak and frail being
>   he must cry out to God for peace
>   he will never be satisfied till then
>   for He gives peace
>   for He gives rest
>   for the ideas and thoughts of man
>   cannot bring peace

"Wow!!" Dink exclaimed when we had finished. "'We sure are weak, puny, little guys, ain't we, Preacha. An so dependent on God fer ever ting. But ya know what? So is da Almandine!---an deys workin' against God!"

We continued rejoicing a while longer, and then I changed the subject.

"What's the plan for tomorrow?" I asked. "Where can we get a bus?"

"Well, somewhere round here der are buses goin' to da New York airport pretty regular. We'll catch one a dose and den take a cab to da hotel."

"Do you think our car will be at the hotel?" I asked knowing the probable answer. "Especially since the Almandine own the hotel? Don't you think it has been long gone---who knows where?"

"Yeah, but I gots an idea, but it needs perfectin' before we can use it!" he said.

"Maybe we had just as well hop a plane home and donate my car to the Almandine!" I offered. "Its pretty obvious that our lives are a lot more valuable than that car!"

"Preacha, gimmie another sayin' to close on!" he asked, changing the subject."

> *Believing prayer will never go unanswered....*
> *Lord, help my unbelief....!*

23

Are They Gaining on Us...?

My times are in Thy hand....

The ride to New York was rather uneventful, but we were cautious in all matters. We caught the bus to the airport just down the road from our motel, and tried to rest as we rode along. At the airport, we took a cab to the hotel not having any idea what to expect concerning our car. Had it been towed? Was it still in the parking lot? If it was, was it rigged with a bomb? The Almandine had to know that it was our car.

I did ask Dink as we traveled if he thought Frankie was really dead, as Billy the cop had said. And also, did he know Geraldo, the new head of the Almandine, again according to Billy.

"Dats hard ta tell!" Dink replied. "Frankie sure was sick when we saw him. As far as Geraldo, yeah, I know him. He was da worst enemy I had in da Almandine---too much competition an bad blood between us!"

I concluded then that if Billy the cop was right, we were worse off than before. Maybe he had been the guy on the council who seemed to want to get Dink. I noted we needed to be extra careful, if that was the case.

"We'se gonna be careful whad ever comes!" he assured me.

When we got to the hotel, we had the cab driver park across the street for a few minutes, while we cased the joint

(I was getting pretty good with gangster language by now!). Seeing nothing suspicious from afar, we instructed the cab driver to pull into the parking garage and drive through it slowly (as we slouched in the back seat) so we could locate our car, if it was there. Much to our surprise, it was still there!

"Sit still, Preacha, wid da door open and be sure da cab driver keeps da engine runnin' while I takes a look around!" Dink instructed me.

He got out, looked in all directions to see if there was anything strange going on which he hadn't seen from inside the cab, and then made his way to the car. He began to look under the car, into the wheel wells, behind the bumpers, etc., to see if it was rigged with a bomb of some sort. He also looked at the engine from below the car as he crawled under it. Seeing nothing strange or unique, he inserted the key in the door (I hadn't seen my car keys since the bunker, but I guessed he had "borrowed" them back from the Almandine).

Gingerly he opened the door, then checked the trunk, and then he got in. He waved us away, just in case there was an explosion, when he turned the key to start it. It kicked off just as if it had been sitting in my driveway. He got out and took another look at everything as the engine warmed up, while I gathered our belongings and paid the cab driver. I guess I didn't give him a big enough tip, because he drove off complaining about stingy people who stiff him. I figured that this was part of life in the big city--- unfriendly, blunt and even rude at times by some, though certainly that did not describe every one.

Dink insisted on driving, just in case they followed us or intercepted us on the streets or highways. That was all right with me---I never had possessed any hankering to be a

NASCAR driver---especially in the middle of New York City!

We made our way through the parking garage, and turned onto the street, and sure enough a car pulled out from in front of the hotel behind us. I looked back trying to get a read on the occupants, while Dink made his way slowly through the heavy traffic. The car following us had tinted windows, so I couldn't see who was driving or anything else about the occupants.

"What are we going to do?" I asked Dink.

"Easy now, Preacha! No need ta get all up tight yet. It might jus' be some big shot celebrity or entertainer. Wait'll I make a couple a turns, and see if dey follows us."

He made the turns in the next few blocks, and sure enough they made the same turns. Could it be a coincidence that they were going our way? Not hardly.

"One more an dat should tell us sometin!" Dink said, as he turned this time down an alley. I only hoped it would exit in the next block. Sure enough, here they came!

"Dat settles it!" Dink exclaimed. "Der onto us now! Hang on, Preacha! We gotta shake em somehow!"

And we were off, screeching around corners and through traffic, missing cars, trucks, buses and people by inches. It was obvious that Dink had some experience in these kind of maneuvers. I was glad he had insisted on driving!

Somehow we lost them, but that didn't mean we were out of the woods yet. We headed for the highway, which would let us travel a little faster, so maybe we could lose anyone else who might try to follow us. I wondered to myself if it was going to be this way all the way home? And then maybe the same at home? Had we opened a can of worms that would never shut, with the Almandine coming after us and our families forever? I surmised that we had gotten past them at the hotel by taking the cab into the parking garage, rather than walking.

Finally we cleared the city and heaviest traffic and were able to move at the speed limit, and I did feel a little relieved. Then Dink spotted them in the rear view mirror. They were coming after us again, and at a break-neck speed. Dink floored it and we were in for a race!

"Dink, we're breaking the speed limit!" I protested.

"Better dan some body breakin' our necks!" he declared as he kept the accelerator to the floor. Soon we were clipping along at ninety miles an hour, weaving in and out of traffic.

"Preacha, sometin's gotta give!" Dink declared, "Cause we'se 'bout outta gas! An dey is gainin' on us! An dey's got guns!"

I began to recite another of my favorite songs:

> *Other refuge have I none,*
> *Hangs my helpless soul on Thee!*
> *Leave, ah! leave me not alone,*
> *Still support and comfort me!*
> *All my trust on Thee is stay'd.*
> *All my help from Thee I bring;*
> *Cover my defenseless head*
> *With the shadow of Thy wing!*

24

Is There Any Friend Like Jesus...?

I have called you friends....

Dink was right. They were gaining on us. Soon they would open fire with their guns. We had ditched our guns the day after we had escaped from the bunker---all except a hand gun Dink had kept---just in case. There was no way we would use a gun on this highway situation, any way, because of fear that some innocent people in another car might get hurt. Our only hope was to out run them---or an act of God's providence.

I turned to see where they were, and all of a sudden instead of gaining on us they fell way back. As I squinted to see, I noticed that black smoke was coming out of their engine.

"Hallelujah!" I exclaimed jubilantly out loud. "Their engine just conked out---blew up or something! They're pulling off to the side of the road!"

I watched them fade into the distance as Dink let up on the gas reducing us to the speed limit as we sailed out of their sight.

"How's that for providence?" I shouted at Dink, I was so relieved and happy. He too was exuberant with joy.

We pulled off at the next exit and pulled into the closest gas station, and our engine died right at the pump! Another work of God's providence! We filled the tank and made another decision.

"Preacha, accordin' ta da map, der's a highway dat parallels da interstate. Why don't we drive it fer awhile, even though its lots slower, cause if dey sends some body after us, they'll be lookin on da interstate."

I agreed with his suggestion, and we took off down the state highway hitting every little town imaginable. But we felt safer. Maybe if they did come after us, they would speed past us on the interstate at their break-neck speed.

It was about two o'clock in the afternoon by now, and Dink suggested that we study the Word to encourage our hearts as we "zipped" along down our "Sunday-drive" kind of road.

I reached for my Job material, and we were into the Word---our first opportunity of that day. I informed Dink that I was going to condense the material, and give only a brief outline (can you imagine a preacher doing that?).

The theme of chapters 15-17 (chapters where Eliphaz speaks for the second time and then Job answers him) is the insensitivity of falsehood answered by the boldness of the truth.

I   THE INSENSITIVITY OF FALSEHOOD   15:2-35

Eliphaz who holds falsehood
    speaks to Job
    with a greater boldness
    with a definite insensitivity
     saying

A. Job is full of wind and hot air   15:2-16

    1. How can Job claim to be a wise man?

a. *Questions for Job   2-3*

> Will a wise man speak empty knowledge?   2
> Will a wise man fill his belly with hot air?   2
> Will a wise man use useless empty words?   3
> Will a wise man speak what does no good? 3

b. *Accusations against Job   4-6*

> You cast off the fear of God   4
> You discourage men from praying to God   4
> Your mouth utters sin   5
> Your tongue is that of a crafty man   5
> Your own mouth condemns you   6
> Your own lips testify against you   6

c. *Further questions for Job   7-16*

> Are you the first man who ever lived?   7
> Were you born before the hills?   7
> Do you limit wisdom to yourself?   8
> What do you know that we don't know?   9
> Don't you know the aged agree with us?   10
> Is the wisdom of God too small for you?   11
> Why are your emotions out of control?   12
> Why are your eyes so fierce?   12
> > so that you turn your heart against God
> > so that words escape your mouth
> Do you think man is so pure?   14
> (What chance does man have?)   15
> > if God doesn't trust angels
> How much more abominable is man?   16
> > who drinks iniquity like water

B. Job Can Be Enlightened If He Will Listen to Eliphaz
    15:17-35

1. <u>The confidence of Eliphaz</u>   15:17-19

    I will show you   17
    Listen to me   17
    I will declare to you what I have seen   17-19

2. <u>The wisdom of Eliphaz</u>   15:20-35

    his wisdom turns out to be the same message
        God judges sin and sinners
            (speaking no doubt of Job)

    a. *the sinner suffers in body and spirit   20-21*
    b. *the sinner suffers judgment 22-25*
    c. *the sinner ignores the warnings of God   26*
    d. *the sinner lives in extravagance   27*
    e. *the sinner lives in upheaval   28*
    f. *the sinner will not be rich or wealthy   29*
    g. *the sinner will be judged   30*
    h. *the sinner's beliefs are vain   31*
    l. *the sinner will die prematurely   32-33*
    m. *the sinner's followers will be desolate   34*
    n. *the sinner has empty hopes   35*

Therefore, Job must be a sinner in light of his condition!

II THE INCONTROVERTIBLE ATTITUDE OF JOB
    WHO HOLDS THE TRUTH   16:1-17:16

Job seeks to answer Eliphaz speech
    he is confident of the truth
        though he is in dire straits
        though he does not understand everything
            that has happened to him

A. Job Rebukes His Friends for Being Miserable
    Comforters 16:2-5

    he tell his friends
        that he has heard all this before 2
        that they are miserable comforters 2
        that their long-winded speeches need to end 3
        that they have a problem if they argue on 3
        that he could talk like they do if in their place 4
        that he could make fancy talks against them 4
        that he could shake his head against them 4
        that he would do differently if in their place 5
            he would encourage them
            he would comfort them

B. Job Is Confused As to How to React to His Trials
    16:6-7

    if he speaks his pain is not taken away 6
    if he doesn't speak his pain remains 6
    whatever he does---nothing changes 7

C. Job Is Confused As to Why God Is Treating Him
    This Way 16:7-14

    God has made him weary 7
    God has desolated his whole household 7

God has filled his face with evidence of sickness
    he has wrinkles which witness against him 8
    he has a leanness of face which bears witness 8
God tears him up in His wrath 9
God hates him 9
God gnashes at him with His teeth 9
God has made him a spectacle before his enemies
    they fasten on him with their sharp eyes 9
    they laugh at him with their mouths 10
    they smite him on the cheek to reproach him 10
    they gather together against him 11
God has delivered him to the ungodly 11
God has turned him over to the wicked 11
God has taken away his ease 12
    He has broken Job to pieces
    He has taken Job by the neck
    He has shaken Job to pieces
    He has set Job as His target
God's archers surround Job 13
    God pierces Job's heart
    God does not pity Job
    God spills Job's blood on the ground
God has attacked Job again and again 14
    God comes at Job like a soldier in battle
      He never quits
Thus, Job is confounded!

D. Job Is Confused As to How to Stop God's Assault
    16:15-17

Job dresses in sackcloth 15
Job sits in dust without strength 15
Job says his face is red with weeping 16

Job has the shadow of death on his eyelids   16
Job has no violence in his hands   17
Job states his prayer is pure   17
(what else is he to do to stop the attack?)

E. Job Still Cries and Hopes for Justice   16:18-17:9

clearly Job knows he is not the great sinner
   that his friends see him to be

1. God, please give me justice   16:18

Job asks that justice will be done
   even if he dies

2. God, you know I am innocent   16:19

even now Job knows that God knows
   that his witness (the truth) is in heaven
   that his record is on high

3. God, you are the one I trust   16:20-17:2

4. God, help me in this hour of trouble   17:3-9

God, give me a pledge   3
   (that my name shall be cleared)
   who else can do this for me?
God, you must be the one to prove my friends   4
   are in error
God, let these friends be judged   5
   in their children

(God, my hour of trouble is so great)   6-9
    You have made me an insult   6
      before the people
    You have made me as one   6
      that people spit upon
    my eyes are dim because of my sorrow   7
    my whole body is but a shadow   7
    my hour of trouble is so great   8-9
      ungodly men would be astounded   7
      innocent men would be aroused   8
      godly men would do what is right   9
        towards me

F. Job Wants His Friends to Leave   17:10-16

Get out of here   10
I cannot find one wise man among you   10
(All is hopeless and I am resigned to my existence)
    my days are past   11
    my purposes for living are gone   11
    the positive thoughts of my heart are gone   11
My false friends are worthless in their thinking   12
    they turn night into day
    they say light is near when it is night
I have no hope in my friends   13-16
    if I listen to them the grave is my house   13
    if I listen to them my bed is darkness   13
    (it does no good to listen to them)
      if I listen to them and say to corruption   14
        that you are my father
      if I listen to them and say to the worm   14
        that you are my mother and sister

> where is my hope?   15-16
> who will see it?
> will it go down to the grave with me? 16
> will hope and I rest together 16
> in the dust?

"Man, what an ordeal!" Dink cried. "God puttin' him through heavy trials (which is God's right)! Job puzzled by it all! Job askin' fer answers, but God is silent! An his stupid friends tryin' ta crush him widda false theology! Boy, I'm sure glad I got a friend like you, Preacha!"

"And better yet," I added, "and a friend like Jesus!"

"Yeah!" Dink laughed. "All of dis and Jesus too!"

We talked a little longer rejoicing and praying and praising. We hadn't seen anything of the Almandine since leaving the interstate. It was about four o'clock by now, and I must admit I was getting hungry. So we stopped at a small town restaurant to get a bite to eat, keeping an eye on the road as we tried to relax a bit.

We finished, paid the bill and went back outside---but our car wouldn't start! Dink opened the hood (I'm not much of a mechanic), and admitted the problem was beyond him. So here we were---fugitives from the Almandine--- sitting ducks without a car were they to drive by.

The restaurant was part of a little complex with a motel and a gas station too, which also had, we found out, a mechanic---but he was gone for the day, seeing it was about 5:00 o'clock by now. The young guy running the gas station told us to just roll the car into the work stall, and we would be the first ones to get service the next day. This we did, and then went over to check into the motel. At least our car was hidden, should the Almandine drive by, and we were snugly hidden also in a motel. God is good!!!

25

Where Are the Almandine...?

When the enemy shall come in like a flood,
the Spirit of the Lord
shall raise up a standard
against him....

We no sooner had stepped inside the motel door, than I saw what appeared to be an Almandine car go by! I called attention to Dink who caught a glimpse of it, and agreed that it was probably them (you don't see very many swanky cars like that in a small town). They were going back north.

Then I saw God's providence in our car trouble. If our car would have started, we would have been going south on that very highway, and they would have seen us as they were going north. God's providential timing is always perfect. I wondered about other times God may have detained me for my own good, yet I had complained about the situation. I asked God to teach me to trust him in every situation.

We went to sleep early that night, hoping our mechanic was an early bird in rising and arriving at his job. Evidently he was, or the kind young man in the gas station had contacted him, because he was on the job about six o'clock. Dink and I were both awake when we saw him drive into the parking lot. I went out to talk to him, while Dink finished getting ready, so we could travel immediately when the car was fixed.

And sure enough, in about an hour he had it running, and we were on the road.

"Well, what'll it be, Preacha?" Dink asked, as he was still driving. "Interstate or back roads?"

I must admit that was a difficult question.

"Dink, its early. Why not try the interstate?"

So we found the next road which shot back to the interstate, and soon we were tooling down the fast lane, hoping to be home by evening. We sat in silence for a number of miles, enjoying the present tranquillity and hoping it would continue. Dink finally broke the silence.

"Preacha, what does ya tink my plan a action oughta be ta find Little Dinky when we gets back home?"

This was the first mention he had made of Little Dinky for several days. I guess we had been too busy fighting the Philistine giants with God's mighty sling shots of providence.

"I don't know, Dink!" I answered. "You know more about the Almandine and what they might do with him than I do?"

"Well, dey'll probably try ta adopt him ta some wealthy family," he explained. "But dis is a big nation, an it would take a miracle ta find him. But I know God is able! But, den I ain't gonna sit home and wait! I know God could do it widout me---He's God. But I know also dat He works through human agency---an dats me an dats my responsibility!"

"Do you think the Almandine will leave us alone when we get home?" I asked with real interest.

"Yeah, probably you, but not me. Dey'll be after me fer life, an I'm after dem too! I jus' gotta outsmart dem! Mosta dem ain't very smart, no how!"

"Do you think we could bring the authorities in to help us?" I asked.

"What authorities? Da police? Maybe da right ones, but ya never know when you'll bump inta an informer."

"What about Troy Medford?" I asked. He was the brother in our church who was a member of the local police department.

"Does you want ta bring him inta all dis?" Dink asked.

"We're in it! He may have some connections!" I suggested.

"Well, we can talk ta him. But whoever gets inta all dis has gotta be ready ta make some sacrifices!" he explained.

"Like what?" I asked.

"Like time, family, safety maybe, job security an much more. Remember, Preacha, dese Almandine boys play fer keeps!"

I had to admit that he was right on that one.

"What about Jimmy?" I asked. "He offered to help and seems to have as much in stake in this as you have."

"Yeah, Preacha, an Jimmy an I knows da system. We'd make a good team."

"Do you really think he will be moving south?" I asked further.

"He'll be here by next week---if he can maneuver around the Almandine ta get here. Pray fer him and Janice, an we better get dem a place ta stay fer a few days."

We made good time the rest of the day, and the closer we got to home, the safer we felt. But when we finally got there, we found out to our sorrow that the Almandine had beat us home!

26

Will God Ever Give Us the Victory...?

Victory comes in the morning.....

Our first day home was spent trying to calm down our wives concerning the long ordeal we and they had been through, especially since the Almandine had come to town just prior to our arriving at home. They had called our wives and made threats, promising they would pursue us further, if we continued to pursue the recovery of Little Dinky. The clear implication was that they would leave us alone, if we left them alone.

Plus, we also had to give a report to our elder board and then to the church, which shocked the life out of some of them. They didn't think such things could take place in the United States of America. I had come to see how sheltered and naive many of us are in our own nation concerning the illegal behind-the-scenes manipulation which takes place in the determination of matters of major import. Power-mongers are always present, and the greater the hunger for power, the more open a man or group becomes to play without any rules or by the rules they set as the game unfolds.

After several days of rest with our families, Dink and I met for Bible study and to seek God's guidance concerning our next step in the search for Little Dinky. As usual, the passage for our study, Job 18-19, was quite helpful and applicable to our lives at this time.

I began by noting the theme of this section where Bildad speaks for the second time, and Job answers him:

THEME---The light of God is given in greater measure to those who are suffering the most, as they trust Him and look to His power in life and eternity.

I   ANOTHER STERN REBUKE TO JOB BY HIS FRIENDS   18:2-21

   A. Bildad Presents Job with a Series of Questions with Each Question Followed by a Rebuke   18:2-4

      1. Question and rebuke number one   2

         How long are you going to torment us with your useless words?
         Let us know and then we will talk sensibly!

      2. Question and rebuke number two   3-4

         Why do you look upon us as dumb animals?   3
         Why are we seen as ignorant men by you?   3
         You tear yourself apart in anger!   4
         Will the earth be removed for you?   4
         Will the rock be moved out of place for you?   4

   B. Bildad Seeks to Convince Job That His Future Will Be Certain and Horrible   18:5-21

      the light of the wicked will be put out   5
         (Job, you will die because of your sin)

the spark of his fire shall not shine   5
    (Job, no hope for you because of your sin)
the light will be dark in his tent   6
    (Job, there is no hope for your family)
the lamp of life will be snuffed out   6
    (Job, God will snuff you out)
the steps of his strength will grow weaker   7
    (Job, you will get weaker and weaker)
the counsel of his own heart will bring him down   7
    (Job, your lack of wisdom will crush you)
the wicked is cast into a net by his own feet   8
    (Job, God's net of wrath has caught you)
the wicked walks into the snare on his own   8
    (Job you walked into this condemnation)
the wicked will be caught in the trap by his heel   9
    (continue to apply all these to Job as above)
the wicked are gripped firmly by the snare   9
the wicked cannot see the hidden noose   10
the wicked are filled with terrors on every side   11
the wicked's every move is followed by terror   11
the wicked's strength is followed by hunger   12
the wicked's side will be plagued by destruction   13
the wicked's strength is eaten alive by death   13
the wicked's confidence will be torn away   14
he will be captured by the king of terrors   14
he will face fire dwelling in his tent   15
he will have brimstone scattered over his place   15
he will see his roots dry up beneath him   16
his remembrance will perish from the earth   17
his name will not be recalled in the street   17
he will be driven from light into darkness   18
he will be chased out of this world   18
he will have no descendants---no son, etc.   19

he will shock all men by his horrible fate   20
this is the dwelling of the wicked   21
this is the place of he who knows not God   21

comments
>   thus Bildad states Job's end is because of his sin
>   >   a horrible death
>   >   a horrible hell
>   >   a horrible judgment
>   >   for all eternity
>   this is the work of Satan
>   >   to frighten us
>   >   to cause us to doubt
>   >   to upset us
>   >   to seek to defeat us
>   >   to seek to discourage us
>   >   with a denial of the truth

II ANOTHER ANSWER BY JOB AS GOD GIVES HIM THE LIGHT OF THE TRUTH   19:1-29

A. The Light Given to Job for the Rebuke of His Friends   19:2-5

1. A question   2

how long will you torment my soul?
how long will you break me in pieces
>   with your words?

2. A rebuke   3-5

you have reproached me ten times   3
you are not ashamed to attack me continually   3
if it is true that I have sinned   4
   my sin remains my concern
you exalt yourself above me   5
you say I am suffering because I have sinned   5

B. The Light Given Job to Correct His Friends 19:6-20

  1. <u>God is the One who has dealt with me</u>   6
     (it is not my sin which has done this)

    a. God has done all of this   6

      Know now
        that God has overthrown me---not sin
        that God has surrounded me with his net

    b. God will give me no justice   7-20

      Behold   7
        I cry that I have been wronged
          but I am not heard
        I cry out loud
          but there is no justice
      God has blocked my way so I can't pass   8
        (add "it is not my sin" on all of these)
      God has sent darkness into my path   8
      God has stripped me of my honor   8
      God has taken the crown from my head   9
      God has destroyed me on every side   10
      God has removed my hope   10
        uprooting me like a tree

God has kindled his wrath against me   11
God has counted me one of His enemies   11
God has raised His troops against me   12
God has encamped in battle   12
   around my tent
God has put my brethren far from me   12
God has set all men far from me   13-20
   my kinfolk have failed me   14
     (keep adding "it is not my sin")
   my best friends have forgotten me   14
   my servants see me as a stranger   15-16
   my breath is offensive to my own wife 17
   my own family hates me   17
   young children despise me   18
   my closest friends hate me   18
   those I love are against me   19
   I am barely alive   20
     my bones cleave to my skin and flesh

C. The Light Given to Job Is So He Can Plead with His Friends   19:21-29

1. <u>A plea to his friends</u>   21-22

Have pity on me   21
   Oh, you my friends
     for the hand of God has touched me
     (it is not my sin)
Why do you persecute me as God does?   22
Why are you not satisfied with my suffering?   22

2. <u>A plea of faith</u>   23-27

    a. a desire for his words to be recorded 23-24

Oh, that my words were now written 23
Oh, that they were printed in a book 23
Oh, that they were engraved 24
    with an iron pen
    on lead
Oh that they were recorded forever 24

    b. a certainty of faith is recorded

In the following words there is a climax of
Job's agonizing struggles---all his agonizing,
all his death fears, all the false accusations of
his friends, all his inability to convince them
of his innocence, all their loud-mouthed lack
of sensitivity, all the desertion by family and
friends, all the lack of relief from his pain and
suffering. Job is given by divine revelation a
powerful certainty from God that there exists
victory even now in the midst of all of his
suffering.

For I know that my redeemer liveth 25
    I need no writing to justify me
    I need no man to argue my case
        for men who follow me
    I have an ever-living almighty redeemer
        He will vindicate me
that He shall stand on this earth
    in the latter day
        there is no doubt who this is---Christ
        but Job will be dead by then, won't he?

that in my flesh I shall see God   26
    though my skin worms destroy this body
    does not this and the following speak
       of the resurrection of Job also?
that I will see Him for myself   27
that my eyes shall behold Him   27
though my heart be consumed within me

Comments
    Christ will raise Job from the dead
    Christ will vindicate him for all to see
    what could be greater than that?

3. <u>A warning of faith</u>   28-29

Thus, clearly someday Job will be vindicated
    therefore be careful how you treat me
    therefore do not persecute me
if you should be saying   28
    we will persecute Job!
       since he is the root of his problem
    you should be afraid of the sword   29
       so that you will then know
       that there is a judgment of God

Final comments
    Thus, Job's present struggles fade as unimportant
      not that he is not still in pain
      but that he realizes
        this life is not the final inning
        the final inning
          will be resurrection and vindication
          no matter what lies the devil tells now

"Wow! What chapters dose are!" Dink exclaimed. "Da game ain't over till da fat lady sings! It ain't over till da final whistle blows! It ain't over till da last shot is taken! An da conclusions concernin' life can't be made till da Great Redeemer Vindicator, our Lord Jesus Christ, stands on dis earth an calls us forth from da dead an vindicates us before all men ta see! Wow!!!"

"Yes," I replied, "The light of the Lord is given most powerfully and clearly to those in this life who are suffering the most, as they trust Him and look to His power to carry them now and vindicate them someday---maybe in this life or maybe not until eternity. Nonetheless, victory and vindication day is coming!"

"Preacha, dat renews my heart ta keep searchin' fer Little Dinky!" he said victoriously. "Perhaps God will vindicate Himself an us in dis life an give him back ta us."

Then he revealed the next part of his plan.

"Preacha, I knows some of da adoption agencies, crooked an greedy people, who work wid da Almandine. I'm goin ta see dem," he explained.

"But won't they just lie to you? What pressure do you have to bring upon them that compares with their fear of the Almandine?" I asked.

"I's got da pressure of da Lord, not dat He is obligated ta me to use it on dem, or not dat I would put physical pressure on dem, but who knows what He might do in our behalf! He's still da mighty God of da Bible! Preacha, I gots a little sayin' fer you!"

We must burn out before we can give out.
We cease to bless when we cease to bleed.

"I guess we been or is ready ta bless a lotta folks now!"

27

Where Shall We Meet You...?

Jesus, Lover of my soul,
Let me to thy bosom fly....

Our time of rejoicing was interrupted by the telephone, something I had not experienced for several days. The party on the phone asked for Dink. The voice sounded rather foreboding and serious.

"Yeah, dis is da Dink!" he answered.

"Yeah!" and then he listened awhile. I wanted to pick up the extension, but it sounded too serious---maybe the Almandine!

"Yeah!" he repeated again.

Then further silence.

Then, "Okay, if Geraldo wants ta see us, den its gotta be in da place we name, after dat last double-cross ya pulled on us---keepin' us captives in da bunker!"

There seemed to be agreement on the other end, but I was a little concerned about them wanting to see "us."

Dink closed the conversation, telling them to call back in about thirty minutes and he would tell them if we both could make it, and where we would meet.

"Well, Preacha, dey wants ta see us both!"

"Why?" I asked.

"Dey wants ta talk over gettin Little Dinky back, but you'se has gots ta be der too!" he explained.

"What do you make of it---a trap, maybe?" I queried.

"Dats why I insisted on us namin' da place!" he explained.

Where should we meet them?" I asked. "I'm glad you rejected the bunker! No way I'll ever go back there! And what will our wives say?"

I knew that Terry wouldn't mind, in light of the fact it might help get Little Dinky back. But I also knew it would concern her. And we had to tell the church.

"Why don't we meet them in Seminary City?" I suggested. "Even at the seminary itself. School isn't in session, but still it would surely be a safe place. Maybe we could take Troy along with us."

"Seminary City an even at da seminary, but we don't dare take a policeman wid us. Dat would spook dem, an we might never get anudder chance ta see Geraldo."

We called the seminary to see if we could get a conference room for the meeting. I had a good relationship with the new regime there, which had taken over after the death of the former president.

The phone call came almost exactly at the agreed time of thirty minutes later. The arrangements were made to meet Geraldo at our suggested time and place---the day after tomorrow at 10:00 in the morning. We gave them directions as to the location of the seminary from the airport, and guessed they would be flying in on a private jet. We would eagerly anticipate the meeting with no idea of what they wanted or how it would turn out. I hoped somehow the bad blood between Dink and Geraldo could be buried.

Then Dink spoke and declared, "Preacha, we needs da Word right now!" I smiled and pulled out my notes on Job, and I organized the material a little differently, but we still got the content of chapters 20-21.

THEME---The failure of false theology and the power of true theology.

This is Zophar's second attempt to straighten out Job, and he gives the same message---Job is a great sinner and that is why he is suffering. Job in turn confronts the real weakness of their theology head-on---that sinners are not always judged in this life.

I FALSE THEOLOGY NEVER DIES---IT JUST FAILS EACH DAY   20:2-28

verses 2-3---the reason Zophar is moved to speak

Zophar is moved to speak again because he is deeply disturbed by Job's speech. He feels insulted by Job's rebuke which reflects on him and he is even convinced it dishonors him. His knowledge forces him to speak.

verses 4-28---the message Zophar is moved to deliver (remember the application is clearly for Job)

4-5---a clear fact
We know from history past two things---
that the triumph of the wicked is short
that the joy of the godless man is brief

6-7---a clear fact without exceptions
Though a wicked man's excellency may mount to the heavens, his head may reach the clouds, still he shall perish in his own dung, and men shall ask, Where is he?

8-9---a clear fact that is a certainty

> The wicked man shall fly away like a dream, and
> he will not be found. He will be chased away
> like a dream of the night. The eye which saw
> him will see him no more. The place he filled
> will behold him no more.

10---the clear fact will affect his descendants

> The wicked man's children will seek to pay back
> the poor---even his own hand will seek to
> get rid of his money in recompense to the
> poor.

11-28---the clear fact will hound him forever

> sin will follow him to the grave   11
> sin will do this though it is sweet now   12-16
>> he has swallowed down riches
>>> but he will vomit them up
>> he has sucked out the poison of snakes
>>> but the snake's tongue will kill him
> sin will rob him of all his labor has gained   17-18
> sin---his sin---is named with clarity   19
>> he has oppressed and forsaken the poor
>> he has violently stolen a house
> sin's results are inescapable   20-28
>> he will have no peace   20
>> he cannot save what he loves   20
>> he cannot save his food   21
>> he will be overcome in his fullness   22
>> he will be assaulted by the wicked   22
>> God will pour his wrath upon him   23
>> he will be struck by a bronze arrow   24

> he will be filled with terrors   25
>> though arrow and sword are removed
> he will lay in total darkness   26
> he will see his tent consumed by fire   26
> he will see heaven rise up against him   27
> he will see the earth rise up also   27
> he will see his increase cease   28
>> in the day of his wrath

> Summary---Zophar is convinced
>> God will judge the wicked man in this life
>>> this is a fact
>>> this is a certain fact
>>> this is a certain inescapable fact
>>>> with no exceptions

II   TRUE THEOLOGY NEVER FAILS---IT WILL SAVE THE DAY   21:1-34

Job asks Zophar to listen to him before he mocks him   2-4
> Hear carefully my speech   2
>> give me that consolation
> Bear with me while I speak   3
>> then mock me if you wish

A.   Verses 4-6---Job's Complaint is not to Man

His complaint is with God. That's why his spirit is is troubled. Take a good look at me and do be astonished. Put your hand over your mouth (if you are shocked)! When I think about all of my afflictions, trembling takes hold of my flesh.

B. Verses 7-16---Job's Complaint to God Is Clear---
The Wicked Do Prosper---But Why?

they live and become old   7
they are mighty in power   7
they live to see their children grow up   8
their houses are safe with no fear   9
they are spared the rod of God   9
their bulls breed and always bear   10
their calves calve and give birth   10
their children dance with joy   11
they celebrate with instruments   12
they spend their days in wealth   13
they go down to the grave in a moment   13
    without suffering
the wicked prosper though they reject God   14-16
    (their easy life seems to lead them to feel no
        need of God)
they said to God   14-15
    Depart from us!   14
    We desire not a knowledge of Your ways 14
    Who is the Almighty   15
        that we should serve Him?
    What profit to pray to him   15
the wicked do prosper   16
    but not because of any goodness
    and I do not agree with their philosophy
        (that they don't need God)
thus Job's complaint to God is clear
    the wicked do prosper

C. Verses 17-30---Job's Complaint to God Is
Tempered

the wicked do not always prosper   17-26
    that they do is a myth
    how often the wicked are snuffed out   17
    how often destruction comes upon them   17
    how often God brings sorrow to them   17
    they are stubble before the wind   18
    they are chaff that the storm carries away   18
    God rewards the sinner---he will know it   20-21
        his eyes shall see his destruction   20
        he shall drink of the Almighty's wrath   20
        he has no pleasure in his family   21
        shall anyone teach God how to deal   22
            with the sinner?
    one sinner dies in full strength   23-24
        completely at ease and in quietness   24
        full of milk---his bones full of morrow   24
    another dies in bitterness of soul   25
        never eating with pleasure
    but they lie down alike in the dust   26
        and the worms shall cover them

Job knows his friends do not agree with him   27-33
    I know your thoughts   27
    I know what you imagine against me   27
        (that I suffer because of sin)
    You say   28
        where is the house of this sinful man?
        where are the dwelling places of the wicked?
            (you say his house has been destroyed)
    But have you never asked those who travel?   29
        Do you not know the evidence?

(The truth is this)
    the wicked are reserved   30
        for the day of destruction
    they will be brought forth   30
        for the day of wrath
(But this is not my situation)   31-33
    no one can point out Job's sin to his face 31
    no one repays Job for what he has done   31
    he is carried peacefully to the grave   32
    he will remain in the tomb   32
    he is welcomed by the clods of the valley   33
        with sweetness
    the men of the earth   33
        follow after him to the grave
        multitudes have gone before him
           to the grave
(But remember the day of judgment will come
    as the wicked are reserved for that day)
(In simple words all wicked men regardless of
    how long they live will face God at the
    judgment)

How do you expect to be able to comfort me   34
    seeing your answers are so full of falsehood

Thus Job is saying
    neither side of the coin is true
        that the wicked will always prosper---false
        that the wicked are always judged now--false
    if we center on the wicked who are prospering
        we conclude the wicked always prosper
    if we center on the wicked who suffer
        we conclude they suffer by God's judgment

if we see any man not suffering
   we will conclude he is righteous
if we see any man suffering
   we will conclude that he is wicked
so what is the answer to the questions?
   why do the godly suffer?
   why are the ungodly prosperous?
   the answers are known only to God
      all events are within His providence
      we must learn to trust in His providence

Dink added his usual "wow" at the end, and then added.

"Den sometimes da righteous suffer an sometimes da ungodly suffer. An sometimes da righteous are blessed an sometimes da ungodly are blessed. We can't draw no conclusions about who is righteous an who is ungodly from some body bein' blessed or sufferin. But in eternity da righteous will be blessed forever an da ungodly will face da full judgment of God forever and ever!"

Then I burst out singing,

Jesus, Lover of my soul, let me to thy bosom fly,
While the nearer waters flow, while the tempest still is high.
Hide me, O my Savior hide, till the storm of life is past;
Safe into the haven guide, O receive my soul at last.
                  Charles Wesley

28

Are We Ready for Philistia's Land...?

His mercy endureth forever....

The next day was a long one, as we waited to go to Seminary City. We were glad for the day's interval, especially since it was Wednesday night, and God's people could meet to pray for us and the entire situation. Thursday morning finally came, and Dink and I took off early for our rendezvous with the Almandine.

I let Dink drive so I could quickly give him the outline of our study of Job 22-24.

THEME: Is God a Legalist?

I   THE VIEW OF ELIPHAZ---GOD IS A LEGALIST AND DEALS WITH MAN PURELY ON A LEGAL BASIS   22:2-30

   A. The Principle Stated in a General Manner---God Deals with Man on a Purely Legal Basis   2-5

     Eliphaz' conviction is stated by a series of questions for Job whereby he states that man brings God no profit by his godliness, man brings to God no pleasure to God by his righteousness, and man gives God no gain by a holy life.

God's judgment has no emotion
   what he does is on the basis of justice
      if a man sins---God judges him
      if a man is righteous---God blesses him

B. The Principle Stated in a Particular Manner---
    God Has Dealt with Job on a Legal Basis 22:5-20

Job is full of sin and he is suffering because of his sin. Job is living and acting as if God does not see his sin. Job is ignoring the evidence of previous wicked men---what God said to and did to them. Job also ignores what God does for the righteous.

C. The Principle Applied to Job---He Must Get Right
    with God 22:21-30

If Job will get to know God, his troubles will cease. If Job will keep the law, his troubles will cease also. If Job does this, he will be blessed once again.

II JOB---GOD'S DEALING WITH MAN IS NOT ON A PURELY LEGAL BASIS 23:1-24:25

A. Job Admits That He Possesses a Bitterness towards
    God 23:2

B. Job Begs to Be Able to Come before God and State
    His Case 23:3-9

He longs to find God. He longs to come before His throne. He longs to state his case. He is convinced God would acquit him. But he is not able to do this.

C. Job Is Convinced That God Will Eventually Acquit Him   23:10-12

God knows the way he is taking. When God has tested him, he will come forth as gold. He has kept God's way and has not gone back from God.

D. Job Admits God's Sovereignty   23:13-14

God is of one mind and who can turn Him? He does what His soul desires. His appointments for Job are being fulfilled. Job is fearful of God's sovereignty.

E. Job Notes That God Does Not Always Judge the Wicked 24:1

F. Job Notes the Sins of the Wicked   24:2-17

G. Job Notes That in the End God Gets the Sinner 24:18-24

Conclusion   25
    Job states that if this is not true
        who will make him a liar?
    Thus
        God does not deal with men
            on a strict legalistic basis
        God deals with men
            in grace according to His sovereignty
            working it all out in His providence

When we were finished, Dink added his comments.

"Praise da Lord, Preacha, what has an will happen ta us in dis whole situation is not any judgment a God on us, but all is within His providence! He loves us in Jesus, an every part a His providence is full a grace an mercy!"

Dink had said it all, and we continued to praise and thank the Lord for all things past and even what might come at the meeting. I couldn't help but ask some questions.

"What do you think will happen?" I inquired.

"Boy, I wish I knew!" Dink replied. "I must say, I don't trust old Geraldo. He's as mean an as crooked as a snake. Watch him carefully, Preacha! Ya can tell when he's lyin' when he assures ya with all kinds of gestures wid his hands an gyrations wid his eyes. He gets all astonished like he can't believe you tink he's lyin.' I hope he's forgotten da time I beat da tar outta him!" Dink said with a smile.

"What over?" I asked.

"He called me a liar! Imagine dat---da big liar callin' me a liar!"

"Where you lying to him?" I asked smiling.

"I don't remember now!" Dink said laughing. "Dat was durin' my B.C. days."

"Gimme a poem, Preacha!" he requested.

Thy right hand shall Thy people aid,
Thy faithful promise makes us strong!
We will Philistia's land invade,
And over Edom chant the song.
Charles Spurgeon
Psalm 60

29

Is This Understanding...?

The greatest sorrow is sorrow wasted....

We arrived at the seminary and checked the room where we would be meeting to be sure it was reserved for us. We had about an hour, so we went outside to wait for them We didn't want to miss them!

Sure enough, about ten minutes past the hour, they pulled into the driveway in one of their swanky limousines. Besides the chauffeur and Geraldo, there were a couple of other hoods with them. Geraldo was about six feet tall, medium build, with slick black hair. He carried himself with an arrogance which made you immediately dislike him, and he spoke in the same manner. When we exchanged a few pleasantries, I could tell there was a coldness between Dink and Geraldo. We led them to the meeting room, which was a fair sized conference room with a big table and nice chairs.

Dink suggested that the hoods (he didn't call them that) stay outside while we met with Geraldo, but at first there was some disagreement. Finally, they left and we were alone with the head man of the Almandine. It was still very tense, but Geraldo began.

"Dink, old friend, I have some bad news for you!" he said coming right to the point. "Your son is dead!" he blurted out.

I thought to myself, he needs a course in diplomacy, but I guess when you're the head man of the Almandine, you don't need any. Who cares who you might offend. And besides, who would ever challenge you?

Dink answered with skepticism.

"Geraldo, ya always was a liar, an you'se lyin' now! You tink tellin' us dat will get us off da trail. Whatsa matter, are ya worried bout da hoods who work for ya tinkin' you'se met yer match in da Dink? Weren't we da first ones ta escape from dat bunker an make it outta der widout you'se guys catchin' us? Whatsa matter, are ya 'fraid of yer reputation gettin a stain on it?" Dink taunted him.

Geraldo held his hands out and made some gestures, and then rolled his eyes as he spoke. It was the style Dink said he would use if he was lying.

"Dink, my man, I'm doing you a favor. I could have just let you find out for yourself. But I have some sympathy for you and I want to make this as easy as possible. Believe me, he is dead! I guarantee you, that is the truth. I have nothing to gain now by lying to you. This kidnapping took place before I took over the Almandine. I would like to end it, and this is the way I chose---an honorable way, a forth-right way!" he assured us---which Dink had said would be another tip-off he was lying.

"What proof has ya got!" Dink demanded.

"Call Janice Masters! She will back me up, because Jimmy Masters was killed at the same time as your son!" he spoke now with the external facade beginning to change. He was almost pleading from his heart now.

"How'd Little Dinky die, an what does Jimmy have ta do wid dis?" Dink asked. "Was you'se guys out ta get Jimmy cause he helped us?"

I noticed a tear sliding down Dink's face. He didn't know whether to believe Geraldo or not, but he was facing the possibility that he might be telling the truth. Maybe, the change of attitude in Geraldo was beginning to convince him.

"We put your son on one of our private jets, and flew to the landing field near Jimmy's town. We didn't know what to do with him, but thought we had to punish him for helping you. So we thought we would scare him a little. We were going to take your son to California for adoption. On the way back, we were going to threaten to throw Jimmy out of the plane in hope that might bring him back in line. Well, the plane never made it to California---it crashed in the Rocky Mountains and was burnt to a crisp---which means everyone in it died---Jimmy and your son included! You can call Janice Masters and ask her. She was at the airport when Jimmy got on the plane. She even played with your son for a few moments when we brought him off the plane to let him run around and expend some energy. Call her---she'll tell you!" Geraldo insisted.

"I will, an right now!" Dink said assertively.

We left the room, and told Geraldo we would be right back. Dink made the call, and I could tell that Janice Masters confirmed Geraldo's story, as the tears became rivers down Dink's face. He did ask Janice if the Almandine had brought her daughter back yet. Then he hung up the phone and buried his face in his hands for several minutes.

I prayed for him and asked God to give grace for this hour---grace to submit, as difficult as it was, to His providence. I was glad that we had been studying Job, as the Lord had laid a foundation for this hour, though one is never ready for such a time as this. And even though one might submit, there was still the question of why, along with tearful eyes, a lump in the throat, and a heaviness of heart.

We went back out to the conference room, and Geraldo saw that Dink had gotten the message. He spoke condolences again. I was afraid that Dink might tear him to pieces, but the Lord constrained him and gave him grace. Then he spoke.

"Geraldo, let me tell ya, dat if it wasn't fer da grace a God dat saved me through His Son, Jesus, I'd tear ya apart right now! Ya may not have been da one who was in charge when dey kidnapped Little Dinky, but ya was da one who was takin' him ta California! Ya better hope dat I never backslide an get away from da Lord fer one second, or I'll be in yer face quicker dan any a yer thugs can save ya, an I'll take you up in an airplane an trow ya out over da Rocky Mountains."

Geraldo looked out the door to see if his boys were near, just in case Dink lost it at this hour.

"Don't ya worry, ya chicken! I'm tryin' my best not ta hammer ya now! But I will make one demand on ya, and ya better keep it or I will come an get ya!" he warned.

"Sure, Dink, whatever you say. Just name it, and you've got it!" he offered frightened out of his wits. Maybe he remembered the last time Dink had "beat the tar out of him." And, it seemed a good bet, that Dink was far more upset now than back then.

"I wants ya ta return Jimmy's daughter now---an I mean now---immediately!"

"Sure, Dink. Anything else?" he asked, eager to get out of there.

"An I wants ya to let dem move down to our city. It may not mean nuttin to you, but Jimmy an Janice was saved da night we spent wid dem, an dey expressed a wish to get outta der an move south wid us."

"Sure, Dink.   Anything else?" he spoke almost pleadingly.

"Yeah, one more ting. I wants ya to set up Janice and her daughter so's dey'll never have ta worry bout der finances again. Ya got dat!" Dink barked out at him.

"An, yeah, one more ting!" Dink added. "I wants ya ta sit here while my Preacha talks ta ya bout Jesus. I'd do it myself under normal circumstances, but I tink you'll understand. Now you sit an listen like a good boy, while he gives ya da gospel."

It wasn't the easiest witnessing experience I had ever faced---in fact it was about the most difficult. But one thing for sure, Geraldo was frightened, and maybe that gave me an advantage. He listened politely, but then rejected the offer of the gospel. I wondered if Dink was going to speak to him as I closed my conversation with him.

Dink did speak but in an unusual way.

As Geraldo was melting all over us in saying good-bye and promising he would do as he promised, Dink floored him with the most fearsome right I have ever seen. It sent Geraldo reeling back all the way across the table and then off into the wall hitting his head with a thud.

"Dat's fer Little Dinky, an just a sample of what you'll get if ya don't keep yer word on dese tings, an if ya don't get off my back. I never wants ta see an Almandine guy in my town again. My wife an I are plannin ta have other kids, an I don't wants to be worrien 'bout you snakes of da earth kidnappin' anudder one. An if I ever finds out ya lied ta me taday, I'll tear yer face off yer skull. An it won't be a funny or happy hour fer you are anyone wid you! Ya got dat message now!" Dink bellowed.

"Sure, Dink. Sure! Thanks for being so understanding about these matters!"

30

Why So Many Mysteries...?

The school of suffering graduates rare scholars.....

We walked to our car, and then watched as they sped down the driveway and were gone. Dink broke down crying again.

"Preacha, I sinned against da Lord, didn't I, when I smashed his face!" he said grievingly. "I sure didn't act like Jesus---da silent Lamb a God!"

How do you comfort a guy who has just lost his only son, and now is convicted because he clobbered the one responsible for his death?

"Dink, I think the Lord will understand this one. If I could have done it, I probably would have beat you to the punch, pardon the pun. And I think you were quite restrained in hitting him just once."

I realized that if Dink had really lost all control, and if I had been called on to try to restrain him from further punches, I could not have done it. I have never seen such strength in any man, regardless of size.

Dink insisted on driving. It was early afternoon by now. I suggested some food---a burger or something, but he said he needed the food of the Word first. So as he drove, I summarized the next chapters of Job, chapters 25-31. And guess what the theme of that chapter was?

THEME---SUBMITTING TO THE MYSTERIES OF GOD'S PROVIDENCE

Introduction   25:2-6

Bildad speaks next and it is a very short speech. Maybe it is a sign that he is getting exasperated with Job. He says that God is sovereign and supreme, and that man is weak and helpless before God. How then can any man be just before God?---a man who is a worm in God's sight! How can Job be just in God's sight? (implied)

Job now gives a very long answer---chapters 26-31

I   JOB ACKNOWLEDGES THE MYSTERIES OF GOD   26:1-14

A. Job Recognizes the Uselessness of Their Counsel   26:2-4

B. Job Recognizes the Uselessness of Their Counsel Is Because They Are Dealing With the Mysteries of God   26:5-14

Who can understand the mysteries of God?

1. The mysteries of God are declared   5-13
2. The mysteries of God remain mysteries to us   14

II   JOB ACKNOWLEDGES THAT MAN MUST FACE THE MYSTERIES OF GOD   27:1-31:40

A. God's Justice Is Questioned by Job   27:2

B. God's Righteousness Will Not Be Denied by Job in
    His Living   27:3-6

    Job says that as long as breathe is within him that his
    lips will not speak wickedness. He will not admit
    his friends are right. He will not deny his inte-
    grity.

C. God's Judgment of the Wicked Will Not Be Denied
    by Job   27:7-23

    1. The wicked have no hope before God   7-12
    2. The wicked will suffer for their sins   13-23

D. God's Mysterious Ways Are Upheld by Job 28:1-28

    1. Man can mine the treasures of the earth   1-11
    2. Man cannot know the wisdom of God   12-28
            man cannot find wisdom   12-19
            man knows not the value of wisdom   15-19
            man's eyes are hidden to wisdom   20-22
            wisdom is from God alone   23-28

E. God's Mysterious Ways Are Not Understood by Job
    in His Own Life   29:1-31:40

    1. There was a day when he was blessed   29:4-6

    2. There was a day when he was respected 29:7-13

    3. There was a day when he lived a godly life---
        full of blessing   29:14-20

4. <u>There was a day when he was considered wise</u>
    29:21-25

5. <u>Now the days have changed</u>   30:1-31

    he is mocked by the older men   3-11
    he is mocked by the younger men also   12-15
    he is in a very serious condition now   16-18
    he has been brought to this end by God   19-23
    he says his godliness is unheeded   30:25:31:34
        by God

6. <u>Now is the day for Job's plea to be heard</u>
    31:35-37

    he asks God to hear and answer him   35-37
    or he asks God to judge him   38-40

Conclusion
    How Job has struggled to understand the ways of
    God!---to penetrate the mysteries of God!---to even
    challenge God to explain his justice and ways. But
    the only answer is to submit to God's providence.
    Yet he struggles with being able to submit to God.

    "Thanks, Preacha! I sure did need dat! Poor Job saw
clearly da mysteries of God, and even admitted dat man had
to face dose mysteries and submit to God.   But it is so
difficult, ain't it, Preacha!" he said as he began to cry again.
    "Your right Dink. Its hard for us to learn that:

        Submission to the divine will is the softest pillow
        on which the troubled soul can recline!!

31

Why Do Beautiful Souls Suffer...?

O Joy that seekest me through pain,
I cannot close my heart to Thee,
I trace the rainbow through the rain,
And feel the promise is not vain,
That morn shall tearless be.

Knowing that Dink had the task of telling his wife this sad news, I tried to keep on encouraging him.

"Dink, do you remember when Job first lost all of his possessions and his children, and what he said at that hour?"

"Yeah, Preacha, but I don't tink I could quote it. I ain't as good as you are in rememberin!" he replied.

"Well, he said the following: 'The Lord gave and the Lord has taken away. Blessed be the name of the Lord!'" I reminded him.

"Yeah, dats good. Da Lord gave an da Lord has taken away. Blessed be da name of da Lord!" he echoed and then kept saying as if trying to memorize it. "I needs ta be able ta say dat about Little Dinky, don't I?" he affirmed.

"And do you remember what else he did at this hour?" I asked again.

"Nah, cain't say dat I remember," he admitted again.

"The Bible says that he worshipped! Do you know what that means?" I asked, stalling my information like he did so often.

"Now, Preacha, you'se actin' like me. I play dat game wid you sometimes!" he said admittingly.

"Well, I'll ask you another question. What is the heart of worship?" I queried.

"Now, Preacha, just tell me!"

"Is not the heart of worship submission? There are many accompaniments of worship (the Word of God, sermons, music, etc.), but is there any true worship of the individual until there is the submission of the heart to the Lord?" I said leading him in his thinking (not that he needed it---actually he was one of the brightest guys I had ever met).

"Yeah, I gets what you're sayin.' We needs ta worship God in submission ta Him. We needs ta see also dat da Lord gave Little Dinky ta us, an now He seems ta have takin him away! Blessed be His name!"

"What do you mean, the Lord seems to have taken him away? Do you still have some doubts about the truthfulness of Geraldo's story?" I asked.

"I told ya he's a liar. It seemed truthful, but I'm goin ta check it out as best I can through da record of da flight plans (da time dey left Jimmy's area an da expected time of arrival in California, da record of da crash, etc.). If der's any crinkle in Geraldo's story, I'll be in his face again. We'll prepare for da worst an praise God, but if God wants ta give him back ta us, we'll praise Him too!"

Then he got pensive for a few seconds and said, "Just tink---Little Dinky may be wid Jesus! Preacha, I wonder what size man he is now in da presence of da Lord? I tink one of the saddest part of all dis is we won't be able ta see him grow up or what kind of a young man he becomes! Won't it be great ta see him in eternity full grown and mature an all dat?"

He began to cry again, and I must admit I cried also. The loss of a child seems so final at that moment, but faith sees a time in the future when we will see Jesus together and when we all shall be like Him.

Before we went to Dink's house, we went by my place and shared the sad news with Terry. We felt it would be best if she was with us when we told Janie. When all three of us walked in, Janie seemed to expect something final, as she broke down and cried her heart out. Dink held her, and Terry held her, as we told the story Geraldo had given us. We prayed together, and then Dink gave her the verse from Job---"Da Lord gave an da Lord hath taken away, Blessed be da name of da Lord."

It is difficult to understand why such beautiful souls as Dink and Janie had to suffer so much. Could all of this really be the will of God? What kind of God would allow this? Where could one go to escape the pit of sorrow and the dungeon of despair? I knew all of these thoughts were or would go through her mind, if they had not already, but I also was confident that His love IS sufficient for every hour.

Oh, Love that wilt not let me go,
I rest my weary soul in Thee,
I give Thee back the life I owe,
That in Thine ocean depths its flow,
May richer, fuller be.

O Cross that liftest up mine head,
I dare not ask to flee from Thee,
I lay in dust life's glory dead,
And from the ground there blossoms red,
Life that shall endless be.

32

Can We Ever Find Closure...?

Self-pity is the enemy of faith.....

Dink spent Friday gathering information by telephone concerning the flight and crash. Sure enough the plane had left the northeast at the time Geraldo said, and sure enough there was a crash in the Rocky Mountains of that plane within the expected time frame. The only other question was whether Little Dinky and Jimmy were on the plane. Janice Masters had assured us that was the case, so the issue seemed settled. Both Little Dinky and Jimmy were dead!

Dink insisted on flying to the closest city of the crash in the west, and taking a helicopter to the crash scene. I tried to talk him out of it, but he was determined to go. Maybe it would bring closure to the whole event. He asked me to go with him, and a few days later we left to go to Seminary City to catch a plane.

On the way Dink drove again, and I went over the material in the next chapters of Job. We were getting close to finishing the book, and I was eager to show the end of Job's suffering, but these several chapters (32-37) were important, so I dared not skip them.

THEME: IGNORING THEOLOGICAL KNOW-IT-ALLS WHO KNOW NOTHING!!

Introduction   32:1-5

Job's friends stopped trying to answer Job because they
thought he was righteous in his own eyes   Now a young
theologian named Elihu feels compelled to speak. He
speaks out of anger against Job and against the friends
because he thinks their answers were lousy. He tries to
appear to be humble, saying he has waited so long to
speak out of respect for his elders. But now he claims
to speak the wisdom they should have spoken.

He acknowledges that wisdom comes from God   6-9
He says wisdom is absent from this discussion   10-14
He claims wisdom will come from him now   15-22
     he is compelled to speak
(So far though he has only shown himself to be wordy!)

I   ELIHU'S INTRODUCTORY STATEMENTS   33:1-7

He gives a plea for Job to listen to him   1-2
He claims that he speaks from his heart   3
He claims he speaks knowledge   3-4
He asks for Job for an answer---if he can give one   5
He asks them to understand his humanity   6-7

II ELIHU'S SUMMARY OF JOB'S STATEMENTS
33:8-11

Job says he is clean, innocent and without iniquity.
Job says nonetheless, God finds fault with him.
Job says God has put his feet in stocks.
Job says God marks all his paths.

III ELIHU SEEKS TO CORRECT JOB'S BASIC STATEMENTS 33:12-33

A. Job Is Wrong in Claiming That God Will Not Answer Him 33:12-13

B. Job Must Be Informed That God Does Answer Man 33:14-24

God answers through dreams 15-18
God answers through pain 19-22
God answers through angels 33:23-24

C. Job Must Be Informed That God Does Restore Men from Sin 33:25-30

God does restore men 25-26
God restores men through repentance 27-30

D. Job Is Informed He Must Keep Still and Learn 33:32-33

IV ELIHU SEEKS TO CORRECT JOB'S MORE DIFFICULT STATEMENTS 34:1-37

A. A Plea to Job to Listen and Learn from Elihu 34:2-4

B. A Plea for Job to Admit His Sin 34:5-9

C. A Plea for Job to See the Truth about God 34:10-33

1. God cannot do evil 10
2. God treats a man as he deserves 11

3. God will not pervert justice   12
4. God is self-appointed   13
5. God is sovereign   14-20
    over a man's life   14-17
    over kings and all men   18-20
6. God sees all things and judges as He wills 21-30
7. God will not meet a man on man's terms   31-33

D. A Plea concerning Job's Sin   34:33b-35:16

1. Job must make a decision   34:33b
2. Job must face the truth   34:34-37
3. Job contradicts himself   35:2-3
4. Job lacks understanding   35:4-16
    sin does not affect God   4-16
    sin is not forgiven just by crying to God 9-16

E. A Plea to Listen a Little Longer to Some Further Important Truth   36:1-37:13

1. a plea to listen a little longer   36:2-4
2. a plea to learn the truth   36:5-21
    God blesses the righteous   36:5-7
    God judges the unrighteous   36:8-14
    God restores the fallen   36:15-16
        (upon repentance)
    God will judge Job for his sin   36:17-21
3. a plea to exalt God   36:22-37:13
    God is now exalted by His power 36:22-23
    God is to be exalted by man   36:24-33
    God is an awesome God   37:1-13

Conclusion
    God must be recognized by Job   37:14-23
        (of course then he will agree with Elihu)

Application

As one reads past chapter 37, one finds no answer given by Job to Elihu. Is it a cultural matter of age? Is it the arrogance of Elihu? Is it that his theology is no different from the three friends' theology?

Elihu seems to speak not because of a difference of theology from the other three men, but because they could not move Job from his contention that this great tragedy was not a judgment upon him because of some deep and hidden and unconfessed sin. Pride seems to be at the heart of all of this, whether he realized it or not.

One theologian has said:
    Tell the younger brothers
        that they may be too big for God to use
        but that they can never be too small.

John Flavel said:
    When God intends to fill a soul,
        He first makes it empty.
    When God intends to enrich a soul,
        He first makes it poor.
    When God intends to exalt a soul,
        He first makes it sensible
            of its own miseries
            of its own wants
            of its own nothingness.

"Wow!" Dink exclaimed, using his regular expression. "Dat reminds me of da old sayin' dat ever body who has got da problem don't have da answers, while ever body who ain't got da problem is full of answers!"

I agreed saying, "Dink, we may not have the answers today, but we will have them someday! Faith doesn't demand answers from God, but God demands faith from us, even when we have no answers from God. Faith is more valuable and rewarding to us than answers."

After the plane trip, we took a helicopter ride of about an hour to the crash scene. Dink quizzed the pilot before and as we flew, though I couldn't hear much, due to the roar of the blades and engine.

The crash sight looked like a charcoaled mess---not much recognizable about it. Dink cried as we hovered over it, but we all had to admit that there would be no benefit in trying to get down to it. Out of respect we threw some flowers down onto the scene, and though the chopper blades blew them all over the crash site, some reached their target.

As we turned to head back to the airport, Dink watched the blackened mountain side as it disappeared from our view, and then he buried his head in his hands and wept profusely. Sorrow and pain do have a way of crushing the strongest of men, and reducing us all to the reality that we are only men and do not have all the answers. Pity the man who goes through sorrow not knowing the Lord!

The next day we arrived home and shared the experience with our wives. We all felt it was over, except for the healing, which might take some years. We agreed to meet for Bible study and finish the book of Job together trusting God to bring final closure from His Word.

33

When Will God Vindicate His Servants...?

Weeping may endure for a night,
but joy cometh in the morning....

We let a few days go by to allow Dink and Janie to deal with the sorrow between themselves. I had told him to contact me when he felt the time was right to finish Job. He called after about a week, and said they were ready. We had them over for supper, and then plunged into the finale of the struggles of a great man of God.

Seated in our living room, with our son Ira in bed for the night (hopefully), I began with some comments about Job's search throughout the book.

I JOB THROUGHOUT THE BOOK CRIES OUT FOR
   ANSWERS FROM GOD---HE DOES NOT UNDER-
   STAND WHAT GOD IS DOING

   he curses the day he was born---ch 3
   he begs God to let him die---ch 6:8-9
   he asks God how he can be right with God---ch 9
        if he is not already right with him
   he acknowledges that God is God---ch 9
        but he longs for an intercessor
   he tells God he knows he is not wicked---ch 10
        but still there is no deliverer or deliverance

he tells God he is full of confusion---ch 10
    he asks why has God brought him to this
he affirms God's providence---ch 12
    but why won't God explain matters to him?---ch 13
he acknowledges God as his salvation---ch 13
    but he asks God to do two things
        to withdraw His hand from him
        to remove the fear Job has of God
he sees that God has brought this upon him---ch 19
    but though he cries
        there is no peace
        there is no justice
    but he knows that his redeemer lives---ch 19
        and will stand on this earth someday
        and Job knows he will stand with Him
he laments that he cannot find God---ch 23
    Oh, that he knew where he might find God
    Oh, that he might come before God's throne
    he would set his cause before God
    he would fill his mouth with arguments
    he would demand an answer from God
    he would demand understanding from God
he acknowledges again that God is providential---ch 23
    He knows the way I take
        and when He has tested me
        I shall come forth as gold
    I have walked in obedience to God
        I have not turned back
    But God is of one mind
        who can turn Him?
        what His soul desires, it does
    He performs the thing appointed to Job
        but Job is troubled at His presence

Dink interrupted me and said, "Preacha, dose are da same thoughts we'se been havin' as we had kinda gone back an forth between da two extremes of faith and doubt!"

I waited for Janie to say something, if she wished, but she only nodded in agreement with Dink, so I continued.

II JOB IN THE LATTER PART OF THE BOOK IS CONFRONTED BY GOD   Ch 38-40

Yet God does not answer his questions of "Why?"
Rather God challenges him:

Chapter 38
　　Who is this that muddies knowledge? 2
　　　　by his ignorant words
　　　　which lack understanding
　　Where were you, Job when I created the earth? 4
　　What are the dimensions of the earth?   5
　　Where are the foundations fastened?   6
　　Who keeps the sea in its boundaries?   8
　　Have you ever brought forth a new day, Job?   12
　　Have you any revelation about death, Job?   16
　　Do you know the size of the earth?   18
　　Explain to me darkness and light! 19
　　Explain to me snow and hail!   22
　　Explain to me the east wind!   24
　　Explain to me thunder, lightening and rain!   25-26
　　What do you know about the heavens? 33
　　Can you number the clouds?   37
　　Can you give food to the animals of the earth?   39

Chapter 39
　　Do you know all about animals giving birth?   1ff

Can you control the wild ox?   9
Did you give wings to the peacocks?   13
Did you give feathers to the ostrich?   13
Did you give the horse his strength?   19
Can you make the horse fearful?   20
    like a grasshopper
Do the hawk and eagle fly at your command?   26-27

Chapter 40:1-2
    Shall the one who argues with the Almighty
        give instructions to Him?
    Let him that reproves God
        give an answer to Me!

Notice God never answers Job's question of "why?"
He only points him to the fact
    that God is God
    that Job is a mere man

III JOB ANSWERS GOD WITH HUMILITY AND A PLEDGE TO SILENCE   40:3-5

Job finally has his time in the presence of God. He has begged God for this hour! He has promised what he would do! He said he would arm his mouth with arguments and demand that God give him an explanation! But now he has no arguments! He makes no demands upon God. He asks for no explanation as to why this affliction has come upon him. He has seen with clarity the message God gave him in the last several chapters.

Note how he answers now:

A. He Acknowledges His Sin   3
    Behold I am full of sin!

B. He Has No Answers for God   3-4
    How can I answer Thee?
    What can I say to Thee?

C. He has Already Said Too Much   5
    Once I have spoken   5
        but I have no words now
    Twice I have spoken   6
        but I will say no more

IV JOB IS CONFRONTED BY GOD AGAIN   Ch 40-41

One would think God would let up on Job!

Chapter 40
    Stand up like a man Job   7
        I have some more questions for you
            and you must answer me
    Will you set aside my will and condemn me?   8
        so you can be right
    Do you have power in your arm like mine?   9
    Can you thunder your voice like mine?   9
    Come on   10
        put on your majesty
        put on your excellency
        array yourself with glory and beauty
    Let me see you bring judgment on the wicked   11
    Then I will listen to you!
    Take a look at that large animal I created   15-24
        he moves and lives by my power

Chapter 41
> Can you control that large animal (the crocodile)   1
> Can Job tame him and play with him?
>> see the rest of the chapter

Notice that God again never begins to answer
> Job's question of "why?"

V JOB ANSWERS GOD AGAIN WITH HUMILITY
AND REPENTANCE   42

Job to God
> I know that you can do everything   2
> I know that no thought can be hidden from you   2
> You asked me why I talk so much   3
>> when I know so little
> Therefore I have to admit it   3-6
>> I have spoken of things I don't understand   3
>>> things far above my head
>>> things I know nothing about
>> I confess now that I only heard about you   5
>>> now I have seen You with my own eyes
>> I hate myself now   6
>> I sit down in dust and ashes   6
>>> to show my sorrow

Thus God never answers the question of "why"
> God's only message to Job is
>> I am God!
>> You must bow to My providence!
>> Be still and know that I am God!
>> That is the place of peace and confidence!

"Wow! Whatta message! Whatta message fer us!" Dink declared repeatedly.

Then finally Janie spoke!

"I feel like we need to pray! I need to confess my sin of not wanting to let God be God. I want to bow to His providence though it is still a painful experience. I want to just be still tonight and let God be God! I want His place of peace and freedom and confidence!"

For a period of time we poured our hearts out to God! We confessed our sin---Terry and I too! We praised God for being the almighty sovereign providential God of all the universe---of all the events of this world---of all the events of our lives---of all the events of the past few weeks---of all the events of this moment---of all the events of the future!

When we had finished I pointed out, "There is one more thing in the book of Job! His vindication!"

We then turned to the forty-second chapter again and saw how God vindicated him in the following ways:

1. Job was restored to his health
2. Job was restored his possessions---twice as many
3. Job was restored his greatness
4. Job was restored children
5. Job was vindicated before his friends
    they were told by God
        that they were wrong in their theology
        that they were to go to Job
            so he could pray for them
            so he could offer a sacrifice for them
6. Job was restored before his family
    they returned to honor him
        (I have often wondered where they were
            when he was going through such suffering)

7. Job was given 140 more years of blessing
8. Job died being old and full of days

From this I drew the following thoughts:

1. Every servant of God that suffers for his Lord will be vindicated by God

2. Every servant of God who suffers will be vindicated either on this earth or in eternity

    a. I pointed them to Hebrews 12 where some of God's servants were vindicated on earth

       some subdued kingdoms   33
       some stopped the mouths of lions   33
       some quenched the violence of fire   34
       some escaped the edge of the sword   34
       some turned to flight the armies of the aliens   34
       some women received their dead to life again   35

    b. I pointed them again to Hebrews 12 where some of God's servants were not vindicated until eternity

       others were tortured   34
           not accepting deliverance
           to obtain a better resurrection
       others had trials   35
           of cruel mockings
           of scourgings
           of bonds and imprisonments
       they were stoned   37

> they were sawn asunder   37
> they were tested   37
> they were slain with the sword   37
> they wandered about in sheepskins   37
>   and goatskins
> they were destitute, afflicted, tormented   37
> they wandered in deserts and caves   38
> all these (died)   39
>   not having received the promise

Dink drew the proper conclusion.

"Preacha, dat means dat dis sinful act of a man which was within da will a God will be vindicated by God some day, either on dis earth or in eternity! Wow!"

This time his "Wow" came at the end of the comments, but it was equally forceful.

"I wonders how God is gonna vindicate us in da sufferin' an death a Little Dinky?"

Little did we realize when or how God would do that very thing!

34

Who Is This Young Man Next to Me...?

He works in mysterious ways His wonders to perform....

In order to finish our story we must advance in history thirty years, even into the twenty-first millennium. By that time I was a professor in a seminary---the one where I had fought the inerrancy battle years ago. Dink was on faculty there also as the head of the evangelism department. Yes, we both had earned our doctorates, and were attending a conference in the San Francisco area when it all began.

I was called home from the conference early because of an emergency in my teaching department, as one of the professors was in an accident on his way home from school. I not only wanted to be with him in this hour, but also there was the need for me to teach. He had also been covering my classes in my absence.

I was late getting to the airport, because I had to rearrange my ticket when the emergency call came. I was the last one to get on the plane. Everyone else was seated, and as I entered the cabin of the plane, one of the large body kind of aircraft, I saw Dink in the back of the plane sitting down already. But how could that be?

Making my way down the aisle, I discovered it was not Dink, but someone who looked almost exactly like him. And in God's providence, my assigned seat was right next to his.

I threw my carry-on luggage into the bin above the seat, and stood there for a moment looking at him. Though he looked like Dink, it was not Dink. He was a much younger man. I sat down and struck up a conversation with him.

"Do you live in the San Francisco area?" I began.

His reply was very precise, and it was obvious he had come from a cultured background.

"No sir, I live in the Washington, DC area. Where do you live?" he asked.

"I live in Seminary City, where I serve on the faculty of Evangelical Baptist Theological Seminary. What is your vocation?" I asked.

"I'm a doctor, specializing in research. I work for the medical agency which recently made a discovery that will revolutionize medicine and medical treatment," he offered.

"Yes, I've read about that. What an honor for me to meet you. What part did you have in that research?" I queried.

I figured he would say that he was one of the many involved in the work, but was I shocked.

"Sir, there were a lot of us involved, but it was my team which solved the medical problem and practice which has puzzled doctors for years," he said modestly.

"Your team?" I pressed further?

"Yes, I headed the team and we had some luck in our work---it always takes some luck in those matters. Some times you just stumble onto something. If we hadn't, some one else would have," he said again blushing.

"I'm not doubting you, but you don't look old enough to have done something like that!" I said with some amazement. "I had always pictured some old fellow like me making such a discovery."

He smiled, not knowing that I was fishing for his age. He accommodated me and said, "Oh I'm in my early thirties! I graduated from high school early, and get a head start in college and then on to medical school, which I finished early also."

I thought to myself, "I'm sitting next to a young genius!"

"Where did you grow up?" I probed without trying to appear nosy.

"In California around Los Angeles. My father was a doctor, so medical work was my interest early in life," he offered further.

A thought had already come to my mind, and I wanted to turn the conversation in that direction to maybe get a clue to answer my questioning mind. I scolded myself, and tried to conclude that my thought was an impossible one. Yet I could not let it go!

"Sir!" I began as politely as I knew how. "Do you mind if I ask you a question which might seem personal?"

"No, go right ahead. If its too personal, I will politely deny you an answer!" he said with a smile.

"Fair enough! Were you reared by your natural parents or were you adopted?" I asked.

A strange look came over his face.

"Are you some kind of psychic or one with extra sensory perception?" he said still looking puzzled.

"No, just someone who is searching for some answers to a situation I experienced years ago," I replied.

"Well, let me answer your question, for I too have had a search in my mind for years. I have been told all my life that I was reared by my natural parents. But I have some memories from the time I was very young which make me sometimes doubt that!" he continued.

"What kind of memories?" I said still searching.

"I have memories of another father who, according to my recollection, loved me very much. We had a very special relationship. I remember having a name similar to his, but I cannot for the life of me remember the name!"

I began to get excited. Could it be that I was sitting next to "Little Dinky?" I warned myself to settle down, and to be careful not to get myself or this young man stirred up over some imagination of my mind. If it was "Little Dinky," I wanted to pursue it, but if not, I didn't want to go any further for his sake mostly, but also for my sake. But how could I determine the truth?

"Maybe these remembrances I have had through the years are just some fabrication of my mind, which it has assiduously refused to reject, because of the coldness of my father," he said with a profound seriousness.

By this time the plane was in the air and we were winging our way across the states. We both settled down to rest awhile, but I found no rest! I was thinking of a way to clearly and quickly determine if this young man next to me held the key to the past tragedy which Dink and Janie had experienced.

I marveled at God's providence which had put me on this plane, as I had not planned to return till the end of the week. And I was glad Dink was not with me or he might have lost it. But how should I precede to deal with this situation? Within hours we would be landing and would be parted, maybe never to see one another again. I needed some key to open the door! But what could I do or say that would give me and maybe him the answers we had been pursuing for years?

35

When Can I Meet My Parents...?

As I continued to pray, I came to the conclusion that the Lord would have to help me on this matter, so I put it in His hands, and then looked for an opportunity to re-open our conversation. When I saw him stir from his rest, I carefully proceeded.

"Are you a married man with a family?" I began.

"Yes, I have a wife and a son!" he responded.

"Oh, what did you name your son?" I asked, and then realized I didn't even know his name.

"We named him Reginald Horatio Bartholomew IV. I guess from that you can surmise that I am the third," he said, almost apologizing for his name.

"Yes, and I assume that your father was the second!" I offered to break the tension.

He laughed and then added, "But we don't call him any of those names---Reginald or Horatio. We call him Little Dinky."

I almost fell out of my seat, and probably would have except I was belted in. Here was the missing piece to the puzzle! I continued playing it cautiously, though my heart was pounding from eagerness to tell him that I knew what had been puzzling him all these years.

"Why do you call him that?" I inquired.

"I really don't know. Not long after he was born, that name just came out almost unconsciously, as I was holding him and marveling at his presence."

Then I knew I had to bring him to an understanding of his mystery.

"Would you like for me to tell you why you call him by that name?" I offered.

He looked at me like I was crazy. How could I possibly do that when I had just met him a little over an hour ago? He sat up straight in his seat, his eyes opened wide, and he urged me to tell him what I was talking about.

"Well, let me ask you some other questions, but trust me as I do. I think I know who your birth-parents are!"

There I had said it, but he was the one who almost came out of his chair now! Seat belts have many uses.

"By all means, proceed!" he spoke beggingly.

"Do you have any memories of being in an automobile with someone hanging on the door as it sped down the highway?" I asked.

"Amazing!" he said. "Yes, yes, yes! But I never could figure that out either! It was that father figure again."

"Do you have any memories of being in a bunker kind of construction?" I spoke with greater boldness.

"Yes, and with this same man being there---that father figure! But how do you know all these things?"

"Do you have any memories of your first airplane ride?" I continued.

"Yes, it was with a man! It seems we left his wife and took off headed somewhere. But I got off that plane and took another plane."

"Was the man named Jimmy?" I asked, not really expecting him to remember that.

"Yes, yes, its coming back now. And I never saw him again after that. He was really a nice fellow! But how do you know all these things?" he queried, letting me know that I had gone far enough, and I had. I possessed now the information that assured me he was Little Dinky.

So I told him the name Little Dinky was from his past, because that was what his father called him during the first two years of his life. And I informed him that his father was the man hanging on the car as it was traveling down the highway as he was being kidnapped. And the bunker was the place where the kidnappers kept his father and me as we were looking for him and trying to rescue him, and they even brought him there to the bunker to visit with us. And I told him that Jimmy was his father's friend who had helped us after we escaped the bunker, and that the plane Jimmy was on crashed. I added that Jimmy was killed in the crash, as far as we knew, and that for all these thirty years we had thought he too was on that plane and died in the crash.

Understandably, he began to cry, and so did I.

"Sir, I don't even know your name, but I want to assure you that these are not tears of sadness, but tears of joy. Please tell me about my birth-parents."

So again I opened my heart to tell him things he had longed to know for years. I told him that his father's name was Derrick Deanaro Smith, but no one knew him by any of those names. He was known by everyone, and I meant everyone, as Dink, da Dink. I told him that his father was originally from the St. Louis area, and he had grown up in a brick-layer's home. He was about five feet eight inches in height, but one of the strongest men physically I had ever met, due to the lugging of cement blocks and bricks as a little kid helping his father. I informed him how his father had become mixed up with the Almandine, explaining what kind of a organization it was, and that he was rising to the top of its leadership, when we met. I explained that we were brought together by the Lord when I was in a scrape with a gang as I pastored a church in Collegetown, and that his father through that relationship had become a Christian. Then he met a young lady named Jane (we call her Janie) at another church in our town, and they were married. While his father was finishing school, he had been born. (I informed him that his father now had a doctorate in theology, and we both taught in a seminary Then I continued). When he was two years old, the kidnapping took place, and the other chain of events unfolded, which caused us to assume all these years that he was dead.

"By the way," I added, "my name is Ira Pointer, and I must say that I am glad to meet you, Dr. Bartholomew, finally! I would call you Little Dinky, but that doesn't seem to be appropriate at this hour."

"And be assured that I am glad to meet you also, Dr. Pointer! When do you think I can meet my parents?"

"Just as soon as I can graciously but persuasively inform them and maybe even convince them that you are alive."

And with that I shared with him the gospel, knowing that Dink would, and that maybe I could plant the seed for its future victory in his heart. I thought in this moment of the happiness of the hour, and I couldn't wait to share it with Dink and Janie!

> *Would we know that major chords are sweet,*
> *If there were no minor key?*
> *Would the painter's work be fair to our eyes,*
> *Without shade or land or sea?*
> *Would we know the meaning of happiness,*
> *Would we feel that the day was bright,*
> *Had we never known what it was to grieve,*
> *Nor gazed on the dark of night?*

36

Do You Remember the Story of Joseph...?

What men meant for evil, God meant for good....

After arriving home, I could hardly wait until Dink got home. I had determined that I would need to tell him first, and then we all (including Terry) would tell Janie. I wanted to ask him to come home immediately, but I would have had to tell him the reason, lest he be overly-concerned to be summoned home not knowing why. After sharing the matter with both of them, we would arrange a meeting of parents and son.

Dink did arrive home on Saturday about noon, and I met him at the Seminary City airport. He hadn't had lunch, and so I insisted that we eat before I took him on home. He had no idea of the joyful shock that was about to come into his life. And I had no idea how to tell him, until a few moments before he arrived. When we had sat down in a remote place in a local restaurant, I began.

"Dink, do you remember the story of Joseph in the Bible?" I began.

He look at me strangely, not knowing where I was going with this, but nonetheless, he replied.

"Yeah, Preacha, he was sold down ta Egypt by his brothers cause of der jealousy!" he rattled off with little interest.

"And do you remember what happened to him in Egypt?" I went on.

"Which part is ya referrin' to, Preacha? Lots a tings happened ta him down dere. What're ya drivin' at any ways?" he chided me.

"Just be patient, and humor me!" I requested with a smile. "The part about God exalting him and then revealing him to his brothers years later. And how they were fearful of his wrath, but he wept because he loved them."

"Yeah, Preacha, I remembers dat!" he answered, still not too happy about my direction of conversation.

"And do you remember what he said at the end of it all?" I asked.

He thought for a few moments with a greater seriousness, since I had finally gotten to a question which challenged his knowledge of the Bible.

"Yeah, he said dat what his brothers had meant fer evil, God had meant fer good," he stated with a growing interest.

"And do you remember what we said when we thought Little Dinky had died---the part about God vindicating his servant someday?" I continued.

He stopped eating and looked me directly in the eye, and asked, "Preacha, is you'se tellin' me dat you'se knows sometin' more bout Little Dinky?"

I couldn't beat around the bush any longer, so I informed him, "Yes, I am, and I am telling you that Little Dinky is alive!"

He couldn't believe it at first. For thirty years he and Janie had been putting their hopes for that to rest, and now were they to be disappointed again with false hopes? Was I kidding him? Was I sure?

Then I told him of meeting Little Dinky (Dr. Reginald Horatio Bartholomew III), and I gave him the entirety of our conversation and of his story, and the proof which I had sought, and that I was absolutely convinced that it was Little Dinky, though that name didn't quite fit him any more.

Understandably again, he broke down and wept, heavy sobs, even to the point of having difficulty in breathing.

"Are you all right?" I asked him, fearing he might be having a seizure.

He gathered his composure, and then said, "I see what ya mean, Preacha. All dat men meant fer evil, God meant fer good. Ya say he and a research team he led made a discovery that will revolutionize medicine? Its so clear now, ain't it? God had a mission fer him, and so He sent him away to fulfill dat mission. God put him in a place where he could get dat kind a background, trainin' and education, so's he could perform dat great work, sometin' he couldn't a done from da background a his birth-parents. An now God is bringin' him back ta us. Its kinda like he's been on a missionary journey, and now he's comin' home. He does want ta see us, don't he? Does he remember us?"

"Yes, he has some glimpses in his memory. He had been trying to figure out for years how these reoccurring episodes in his memory fit into reality. Believe me, he was as happy to know of you as you are to know of him. He is eager to meet you all also!"

He stopped crying now and began to rejoice, pumping his fist into the air saying, "Wow, God's servants has been vindicated by da Lord! God's servants has been vindicated by da Lord! Just like ya said thirty years ago, Preacha---someday it would happen, either in heaven on dis earth. God in His mercy and grace and glorious providence is lettin' it happen on dis earth. Wow! Hallelujah!!"

He kept on praising.

"What providence, Preacha! What odds are der dat you an him would be on da same plane? Of all da planes dat fly in da world or even in da states, what odds a bein' on da same plane? And even if on da same plane, what odds dat you an him was seated next ta each other? Talk bout providence! When can we meet him?"

"Well, if it is convenient, he wants to fly down with his family the day after tomorrow! I say again, he is as eager to see you as you are to meet him. I suggest that you let Terry and I meet him at the airport, and then bring him to your house. It will be such an emotional meeting, that I am not sure a public place would be the best location."

He was in agreement, and then began to ask other questions.

"Is he a Christian? If not, God's gonna save him!"

"He's been witnessed to!" I replied.

"Ya mentioned his family! Kids?"

"Yes, a wife and one little boy that he calls Little Dinky."

He smiled and cried again. Its not often that you see someone cry while they smile!

"Preacha, let's go tell Janie! But I'm gonna let you do da talkin' cause I would bust out cryin' an not be able ta get a word out," he declared.

"Yes, but let's take Terry with us. She's waiting for us to pick her up on the way to your house!"

Dink floated out to the parking lot. He probably could have gotten home without any vehicle of conveyance, and beaten me at that, as I traveled in my car. Thirty years of pent up emotions were venting in joy, and this was just the beginning of the rejoicing!

37

How Do We Relate to a Stranger...?

Unbelief asks how; faith answers one word---God....

The next question was how to tell Janie. She was a very sweet girl, an outstanding Christian, but far from being as bold or as strong in faith as Dink. He felt threatened by no one! But what if she felt threatened to know her son, whom she hadn't seen in thirty years, was a young genius who had solved a major medical problem of the world? What if she felt their humble home was far too humble compared to the mansion in which he had been reared? What if she flinched at the thought that he had been in the presence of the greatest people and minds of the world? None of this mattered to Dink! But could it threaten her so much that she would be hesitant to meet her own son? I'm not sure it would not have threatened me had I not known his humility!

We pulled into the driveway, and she was at the door to meet us!

"What a pleasant surprise!" she exclaimed. "I wasn't expecting you both!" she rejoiced, not knowing that wasn't the only surprise.

She invited us in and made us feel comfortable and welcome. Dink was about to go out of his mind, having to wait for me to share the news. So after sharing some pleasantries, I began.

"Janie, we have something to share with you that is good news, but it is not easy to tell!"

"Go ahead, Pastor!" she said, still calling me pastor though I was no longer her pastor.

"We are rejoicing and we know you will rejoice with us, though the news will surprise you!" I said, not sure whether I was preparing her or myself.

"Why all the mystery?" she asked. "You can tell me what the news is!" she assured me.

I couldn't stall any longer.

"Little Dinky is alive!" I said as plainly as possible.

She too had a look of unbelief as had Dink when I first told him. And understandably again, she began to cry, so we all began to cry!

"But he would be over thirty years old now. Where has he been all these years? Why didn't we know about it sooner? And what has he been doing and what is he doing now?" she thought out loud.

I gave her the full story. His background and life. His brilliance, even that he was a young genius. His medical research. His questions and remembrances as he grew up. Our being on the same plane by God's providence, and even in seats next to one another. Our full conversation. His eagerness to meet his birth-parents.

She kept on wiping tears throughout the sharing of the news with Dink holding her hand and crying too. I realized her facing of the matter was different even from Dink's experience. Here was a young adult she would soon meet, whom thirty years ago she had carried for nine months in her body, to whom she had given birth, whom she had cherished and nurtured and granted all her effort and time for about two years as he had been in those days totally dependent upon her, and now he would re-invade her existence as a total stranger. She had been given no opportunity to mold and shape his life, to teach and train him in his thought, or to build a relationship between their hearts. How do you relate immediately to a total stranger that you knew at a young age, but who is now almost completely the product of a different culture and environment? Yet as his birth mother, there seemed to be very high expectations of immediate relationship!

I had known Dink long enough to know he built relationships very quickly. In fact, he never met a stranger. He could instantly relate to anyone. Perhaps, though, there was a danger for him in the meeting of his son, because neither of them had ever been and never would be in such a meeting as this one.

I sensed a possible bitterness when Janie said, "What about this medical doctor father who paid millions to the Almandine to adopt him? And what about the Almandine who lied to us? Where is old Geraldo now? I wonder what he would say if we confronted him? Dink wouldn't have to punch him out this time---I would!"

I could tell that she wanted the meeting, though there was no guarantee it would be a smooth one. We shared the Genesis 50:20 passage about what men meant for evil, God meant and used for good, and we also sought to emphasize the providence of God in the whole matter, and that we must submit to Him. And then we prayed together!

I knew it would be a difficult time for her waiting for the reunion---she was hurting and healing, and restoration of the relationship would take time.

Plus, I knew she had raised some issues that might not go away in Dink's mind very quickly---the parents by adoption and the Almandine. Could he let those matters rest, or would he seek further closure in these areas?

Who Can Believe
What God Hath Wrought...?

We can wait till He explains,
because we know that Jesus reigns....

The time waiting for the reunion went quickly for us, but I am sure it was not quick enough for Dink and Janie. As Terry and I waited at the airport, a new thought came to my mind---what if Reginald (that name didn't sound quite right, but I figured I had better get used to it) had married some snobbish rich girl, who would be against or even lukewarm about Dink and Janie. And further, how would either of them take Dink's butchering of the English language?

When they stepped out of the corridor which led to the plane, I was shocked again. The new Little Dinky, who was about the same age as his father when he was kidnapped, looked just like him. This was incredible! Truly, another Little Dinky!

It was a warm greeting, and I already knew that Reginald was friendly and easy to meet, but I was surprised that his wife was every bit as open to us! We found out she was not from a wealthy home, but from a very humble background. Reginald laughed as he said that all the elite young debutantes he had grown up with and gone to school with had for the most part disgusted him. It wasn't until he had met Linda that he had any interest in marriage, though that decision had not pleased his adoptive parents.

As we drove, I thought I had better warn them about Dink's language. I told them he talked like a gangster, but those days were far gone. They laughed about it, and said nothing like that would bother them. In fact, they at times got weary of the pretentious language of the super-sophisticated societal clinging vines and ladder climbers.

I thought to myself, one problem after another is being solved and other positives are clear---Reginald has married an outstanding young lady. That should go a long way in re-establishing the relationship. Plus, he himself is a very humble young man, even though he is a genius. Plus young Reginald (the new Little Dinky) looks like his father and grandfather. Plus, they won't mind Dink's language.

When we pulled into the driveway, I could sense a tenseness building. While we were walking up the steps to the front door, it opened, and Dink and Janie stepped out. We let our visitors go first, and when they reached the porch, they all embraced in one large and long hug. Tears flowed from all eyes---including mine and Terry's. It seems they stood there for a small eternity as the emotions of thirty years spilled out all over the porch.

"We didn't tink we'd ever see ya agin!" Dink spoke through tears, breaking the silence. "What a gift a God. Da Lord gave, an da Lord took away, but now He has sent ya back to us with even more---a wife and a son! Oh, praise da Lord!"

"I've searched my mind for years for clues to find my past," Reginald said, "but nothing I did could ever open the door to it. God had to be the one who did it!"

Then he told us something that just melted the whole scene even further and united hearts for certain.

"Linda is a new Christian, Mom and Dad, and she's been witnessing to me. Plus, Dr. Pointer told me of Christ on the plane. How can I turn Christ away now in light of all of this? Could we begin our relationship anew by my confessing to you my faith in Jesus Christ the Son of God as my Lord and Savior? I know it has been your prayer through the years which has brought this to pass!"

By that time Terry and I were on the porch joining in on the hugging---we already were bawling our eyes out. We all joined in an even larger hug-mass as we prayed thanking God for what He had done, and especially for saving Reginald.

We spent the rest of the day fellowshipping, with the three ladies knitting their hearts together as they scurried around the kitchen preparing a meal and talking away. And we men spent our time talking too about many things--- much about the Lord and also a full discussion about the kidnapping, and our contact with the Almandine, and our escape from the Almandine, and then what had happened in Reginald's life those thirty years. The ladies kept saying, don't tell every thing, or you'll have to repeat it at dinner. Little Dinky went from person to person, seeming to enjoy the day as well.

But there were still a few items to deal with which we seemed to steer around---the Almandine and Reginald's parents by adoption and the relationship between the two. Maybe that could wait until another time---or maybe forever.

Or maybe the Lord would solve those problems!

What about the Adoption...?

This my song through endless ages,
Jesus led me all the way....

The issue of the Almandine did not have to be pursued by us (in God's providence again), as unexpectedly, they came to us. Once again, it was by way of a telephone call, and one of the hoods informed us that Geraldo wanted to speak with us. Again we insisted that it be on our turf, thus we agreed to meet at the seminary conference room, as we had met thirty years previously.

As we drove to the campus, I asked Dink if he was surprised that Geraldo was still alive.

"Nah, he's 'bout my age, and I'se still alive, so no big deal dat he's alive!" he explained.

"What do you think they want?" I inquired.

"Oh, maybe deys been informed dat we'se made contact wid Little Dinky, I mean Reginald (der I go agin, Preacha, havin' trouble wid dat name). Ya can't call a guy Little Dinky when he's thirty years old, can ya?"

"What else could it be?" I asked.

"Well, maybe deys 'fraid of us! Or maybe deys trying ta protect Dr. Bartholomew. Or maybe dey tink we might go after some middle man---da middle man in da adoption," he explained. "We'll soon know!"

I noticed that as the Almandine guys drove up that they had a set of younger hoods. For the first time, I wondered what happened to all hoods who grow older? Do they retire, or just not get old---maybe hoods die young.

Geraldo was helped out by his boys. I knew he would look older, but not this old! Thirty years as leader of the Almandine had done a job on him. Dink and I had aged, but Dink may have been wrong---it looked like a big deal he was still alive.

They wheeled him into the conference room, and we insisted that the hoods leave.

"Hello, Dink! How are you?" Geraldo began with a stiff attempt at a smile. "And you, preacher, how are you? Is it true that you, Dink, are Dr. Dink now, and that you teach at this seminary."

"Yeah, dats all true! And how are you doin'? Ya don't look too good, Geraldo!" Dink stated bluntly. You could always depend on Dink to get to the point.

"Well, I've been sick. Its pretty tough being the head of a mob and getting old. It seems like there are so many waiting in the wings to take your place. And they aren't very patient. You have to keep beating them off---eliminating the competition in one way or another!" he explained.

"Yeah," Dink countered, "da Bible says dat da way of da transgressor is hard."

"Well, enough of the chit-chat. Let me tell you why I wanted to see you. I understand you know your son didn't die in the plane crash. I understand also that you might want to come after me or Dr. Bartholomew, holding us responsible for the adoption. Well, let me explain to you what happened. It wasn't my fault. I didn't even know that your son was not in the plane crash. I assumed he was there with Jimmy. Honestly! I didn't find out until several years later, and then I didn't see any need to try to straighten it all out. You believe me, don't you?" he spoke pleadingly.

"Listen, Geraldo, it don't make no difference now! God knew 'bout it den, an God knows' bout it now, an you'll answer to Him an not me. He knows if you'se lyin' or tellin' da truth. He'll judge ya fer yer sins, and He's got a lot more power and knowledge ta do it right dan I has. So don't be 'fraid a me---ya'd better fear God!" he said as he got up out of his chair.

Geraldo flinched as if he remembered our last meeting, and I'm sure he did, when Dink decked him. But Dink told him he was just stretching a little bit.

"In fact, Geraldo, I wants ta apologize fer deckin' ya when we met wid ya da last time! I shouldn't a done dat. I wants ya ta forgive me for it!" he asked repentantly.

Geraldo was shocked! Dink asking forgiveness---impossible. Not Dink!

"I means it, Geraldo. I knows yer just an old lost gangster, and you'll burn in hell unless ya get saved. But I'm a Christian, and I knows better, an I shouldn't do tings like dat. It didn't cause me ta lose my salvation or nuttin' like dat, but it wasn't actin' like Jesus, and dats sin."

Geraldo sat speechless.

"Now," Dink continued, "tell me about da adoption! Who was responsible fer it if you weren't, an what place did Dr. Bartholomew have in it? An how much did he pay you'se guys fer Little Dink?"

"That's a lot of questions, Dink. I'm not sure I can answer them all!" he plead indirectly.

"Well, let's just give it a try, how bout!" Dink insisted. "Ya ain't gettin' outa here till ya gives us some answers! Jesus won't mind if I detain ya, but He won't let me hit ya!"

Who Heads the Almandine...?

Sometimes we serve God by waiting....

When pressed further by Dink, Geraldo opened up and began to talk, sharing with us the full story. He told us that he was not the real head of the Almandine, and neither had Frankie been the ultimate authority. The organization has a visible front man, one that every one thinks is the final power of decision, but that man is only a puppet to the ultimate person of power.

"That's something, Dink, that you never knew during your time in the organization!" Geraldo asserted.

Dink's term which was usually reserved for theological matters, was used at this point!

"Wow---does dat ever surprise me!" he marveled. "Okay, den, who is da real authority of da organization?" Dink demanded. "I guess dat person was da one responsible for how we was treated, Little Dinky's kidnappin', da death a Jimmy Masters, an on an on."

"Yes, but do you realize what it will cost me if I tell you who that is?" Geraldo asked. "It will cost me my life--- unless I can take that person down!" he said speaking with some fright!

"Ya don't wants ta take him down just so you can be da big man, do ya?" Dink probed.

"No, I want out of this! Out forever! No more! I'm sick of this organization. I've been sick of it for years. Do you know, Dink, if I would have gone the route you went in those early days, I'd have a life now. Your life almost persuaded me to become a Christian!" he pined.

"Well, it ain't too late!" Dink said as he tried to witness, but Geraldo cut him off.

"Yes it is Dink! Just help me bring down the Almandine, and I will be satisfied! I will have peace. I can die in peace. Please help me, Dink!" he pled.

"Well, ya may die in peace, but ya won't have any peace after death unless ya get saved before ya die!" Dink shot back.

Geraldo had his mind made up and seemed to ignore him! He seemed eager to tell us the head of the Almandine, if we would help him bring them down.

"Please, Dink, promise me you will help me eliminate the Almandine!" he pled again.

"Well, first, what plan does ya have ta do dat?" Dink asked.

"I have documents in the trunk of that car out there that will put every member of the Almandine behind bars, but especially the head man---he'll be gone forever!" he promised.

"Plus, Dink," he continued, "I think you, of all people would want this man behind bars, so he could do your family no further harm!" he added, as if he was baiting a hook.

"Okay, ya gots my help on dese conditions. First, if you'se got da documents. Second, if ders really a reason I wants dis guy behind bars---dat is, if it matters ta me. Third, if ya can prove ta me dat you'se on da level. Geraldo, ya knows dat you've been a liar ever since I've known ya. Convince me dat you'se tellin' da truth now!"

"Which order do you want me to follow?" Geraldo asked.

"First, tell me whose got control!" Dink directed.

"Okay, but brace yourself. Once you find this out, you'll not need any thing else to convince you to help me. The head of the Almandine has been for years the Bartholomew family---and they are still in control. Today, the head is Dr. Reginald Horatio Bartholomew, Jr.---the man who adopted your son! His father, Dr. Reginald Horatio Bartholomew, Sr. was the founder of the organization, and the head of it when you were in it. Is that too confusing? The organization has been a means to make that family very rich, powerful and influential over the years."

On that one I said, "Wow!"

"And that's not the whole story!" Geraldo said. "Your son, Dr. Reginald Horatio Bartholomew III, is the next in line to head the organization. That's why they kidnapped him---either to get you to give up this religion business and lead the Almandine (which you refused to do), or to train him to lead the organization. But they could never seem to corrupt him with the lust of the flesh nor capture him by the wiles of the world---money, power, influence, etc. Though he was not a Christian, there seemed to be a wall around him that kept them from getting their clutches into him. He had an incorruptibleness about him they couldn't figure. They had always been able to manipulate and corrupt men before---but not your son"

"Hallelujah!" Dink declared loudly. "Dat was da power of our prayers all dese years. We asked God ta protect him an keep him, if he was still alive!"

"Well, something kept him," Geraldo marveled "But they never give up. And now they figure that he knows too much, that if they can't sway him, they will eliminate him. And he has informed them that he has made contact with you. That will pretty well settle it! Its just a matter of days until he's gone in one way or another!"

Dink then demanded all the evidence! So the hoods brought in the boxes. It was a trunkful! We inspected it, and Dink acknowledged that the records were legitimate and that it would bring down the Bartholomew family.

"One final thing, Dink. What authorities are you going to give this stuff to, and do you think they could give me clemency and a new identity?"

"Ya knows I can't make any promises, Geraldo. But ya got my word, dat since ya brought dis stuff ta me, dat I'll do what I can!" Dink assured him. "We'se got a friend in da FBI dat we'll contact!"

The parting was cordial, because Dink knew that Geraldo had done him a great favor. Dink urged him to get saved, but there was no encouragement that he would.

When Geraldo was gone, we called Troy Medford, the FBI agent. Dink marveled at the providence of God---how I had won Troy to the Lord years ago during the battle at First Baptist Church in Collegetown. He was from the family that had beaten me badly because of their hatred. He was a local policeman then, and now he's an FBI agent--- God's providence! He noted that we can see God's providence a lot clearer, when we look back on it, than when we are going through it. He then gave me a poem:

When I cannot understand my Father's leading,
And it seems to be hard and cruel fate,
Still I hear that gentle whisper ever pleading,
God is working! God is faithful! Only wait!

Who Keeps the Key...?

He keeps the key....

The time has come for us to bring this study and story on providence to a close. The following events came to pass as a result of the meeting between Dink and Geraldo as explained in the last chapter.

The FBI through Troy Medford was extremely interested in the documents which had been given us. We worked out a deal, which enabled Geraldo to receive clemency and a new identity. But within a year, word came to us from Troy that he was dead. He had shot himself. It seems the new identity had not brought him the peace he had hoped for. How mistaken men are that they can find peace without facing and dealing with their sin.

The Almandine organization was brought down. It was a painful experience for Dink to have to inform his son that his father by adoption was so corrupt, but he finally came to that understanding. The relationship between him and Dink strengthened in the years to follow until Dink finally went to be with the Lord (but that is another story for the future). I must admit that life was less threatening with the Almandine gone, for we had lived for a number of years with an uncertainty of when they might come after us again. And they would have, had it not been for the Lord's protection and providence in getting us the documents. He got them to us---we did not go looking for them.

And Janice Masters died a year or so after the Almandine were brought down. She too felt vindicated for the death of her husband Jimmy. She and her daughter had moved to our city back at that time of his death, and the daughter married a preacher. We talked of Jimmy often and of his help which saved us from the Almandine, but which finally brought his death. The plane in which he died had been sabotaged for the purposes of eliminating him and making us think that Little Dinky was dead also.

Reginald Haratio Bartholomew III (Dink's son) changed his name to Derrick Deanaro Smith, Jr. and Little Dinky's name was changed to Derrick Deanaro Smith, III There were news story reports for a number of weeks when the Almandine fell, and finally, it was revealed that the older Bartholomew headed it. Dink's son was a household name because of his medical research.

We all marveled in the years to come of the glory and reality of God's providence---that is, that He is in control of all things. Why is it so hard for men to believe in His providence? If He is not in control, who is? One certain man? The devil? Each man? The Almandine of the world? Isn't that a scary thought? Certainly there is a mystery to His providence---how man can be responsible and God be sovereign. But the Bible teaches both and we must hold to both. God is a providential and sovereign God, and man is a responsible creature. That is the Biblical witness!

Why would men rather have man in charge than God? Why would men think this subject must be fully explainable to man's puny mind. Remember, let God be God! What basis is there for letting man be God?

Finally, Dink asked me if I ever recorded this story to include the following poem---one he had learned and had shared with me several times:

Is there some problem in your life to solve,
Some passage seeming full of mystery?
God knows, who brings the hidden things to light.
He keeps the key!

Is there some door closed by the Father's hand
Which widely opened you had hoped to see?
Trust God and wait---for when He shuts the door
He keeps the key!

Have patience with your God, your patient God,
All wise, all knowing, no long tarrier he,
And of the door of all thy future life
He keeps the key.

Unfailing comfort, sweet and blessed rest,
To know of EVERY door He keeps the key.
That He at last when just HE sees 'tis best,
Will give it THEE!